GARY OF A HUNDRED DAYS

ISABEL MURRAY

Copyright © 2022 by Isabel Murray

All rights reserved.

No part of this book may be reproduced in any form or by any electronic or mechanical means, including information storage and retrieval systems, without written permission from the author, except for the use of brief quotations in a book review.

This is a work of fiction. Names, characters, places, and incidents either are the product of the author's imagination or are used fictitiously. Any resemblance to actual persons, living or dead, events, or locales is entirely coincidental.

First paperback edition August 2023

GARY OF A HUNDRED DAYS

The Kingdom of Estla is in turmoil. Power plays, intrigue, and plots seethe in the corridors of power. And Gary of a Hundred Days, Last of the Tyrant Kings is...well, he's pretty offended, actually?

Tyrant?

Seriously? Who is making this up?

Gary said no thanks, don't want to be king, and they dragged him away from all he's ever known and stuck a stupid crown on his head anyway.

As far as Gary's concerned, all that political intrigue can go ahead and keep seething without him. He didn't know or care a thing about it when he was the unwanted son of a backwater lord. He definitely doesn't care about it now they tried to kill him and he's on the run.

Minor problem: he managed to escape, but he's all out of ideas. It's dark, it's raining, he's in the middle of nowhere, and there might be bears. In fact, he's pretty sure one is following him.

Luckily for Gary (it's about time he had some *good* luck) his ex-stable master tracks him down, and it turns out that Magnus has more than a few interesting ideas about Gary and his future.

More specifically, about *their* future.

Gary of a Hundred Days is a low-angst fantasy romantic comedy in which a sheltered ex-king undergoes quite the awakening at the hands of his rugged ex-stable master, and everyone's way more interested in kissing and romance than in all that rightful heir to the throne business.

Somehow, despite an entire kingdom wishing him dead, it's starting to look like Gary might just end up with a happily ever after?

(Unless that really is a bear following him.)

1

Once, I read a book about a breed of wild goats who live in one of the mountainous kingdoms to the east. Valdran, I think.

When threatened with any kind of danger, these goats turn rigid and topple over in a dead faint.

The author didn't give any detail on how well or not this fainting strategy usually works for the goats, and at the time of reading, I remember thinking that it was unlikely to be useful in terms of survival.

I couldn't imagine that the predator that had caused the fainting fit—wolf, bear, or troll—would look down at the swooning goat and think, *Oh, darn. It's dead already? Where's the fun in that?*

Surely they'd be more likely to think, *Oh, happy day. Dinner is served!*

But since the goats had developed this strategy, and survived to breed vigorously enough that they were considered absolute pests by any local farmers trying to raise crops, it must have had a fairly decent success rate.

I can tell you that for me, at least, it worked a treat.

∼

I came to facedown on the marble floor, with my neck at an awkward angle.

I frowned and blinked at the time-worn pits and cracks in the ancient stone that no amount of buffing would ever smooth out.

Where...?

My hearing popped and rushed back with a jangling roar of sound: laughter, music, and voices raised high in jubilation. It was, I registered, at a slight distance, not in the same room as me. The throne room, then, my muzzy brain supplied.

"Down with Gary of a Hundred Days, the Last of the Tyrant Kings!"

Indignation wiped the muzziness away like a bucket of cold water.

What? Gary the *What?*

A roar of approval went up. I flinched at the percussive *pop-pop-pop* of corks.

Hurried footsteps clicked over the marble floor, coming my way. More than one set.

I squeezed my eyes shut.

They came closer and closer.

I braced myself to be grabbed, hauled upright and...well, I quailed to think what would come next.

I was still quailing when the footsteps briskly clicked past and were absorbed into the noise of the party everyone but me seemed to be having in the throne room.

As slowly as I could, I cracked my eyes open and took stock.

I remembered heading for the door. As usual, the First Minister, Drusan Visik, was there by my side, guiding me with a hand at my back. Lulling me into a false sense of security, I now realised. I should be facing the doorway head-on, but when I raised my head juuuust enough to look, I was looking at a wall. I was still in the council chamber, but I'd been dragged to one side.

I froze again and closed my eyes as footsteps returned from the throne room. The tendons in my neck quivered. I didn't dare lower my head, terrified that any movement would draw attention. The footsteps passed.

I cracked my eyes open in time to see three servants with trays of empty goblets vanish through the door.

What the hell was I supposed to do now?

"Down with Gary!"

I gritted my teeth. How many times were they going to—

"Huzzah for Drusan the Liberator! The bravest of us all. The man who did what must be done! For the good of the kingdom!"

Huzzah for *Drusan*?

The latest toast rang out, loud above the noise of the party. The booming voice belonged to one of Drusan's fellow ministers, and one of his staunchest supporters. There weren't all that many left. His inner circle of close friends had thinned out somewhat as the assassins kept missing their target (me) and getting the wrong men (them).

One of the violins playing a jaunty, triumphant tune squeaked. There was, for a single trembling moment, a break in the celebrating.

Then the cry was taken up. First by a couple of people, then by a handful, and then they fell in, one after the other, until they were shouting with a single voice.

Down with Gary! Huzzah for Drusan!

Right. I wasn't going to lounge around and listen to this crap.

Drusan the *Liberator*?

How about Drusan the Murderer? How about that?

I clenched my fists and forced the anger, betrayal, and sheer overwhelming panic down as far as it could go. I'd had plenty of practice at repressing these emotions over the last three months—*three months, Drusan*. It wasn't a hundred days, actually.

I knew that for a fact, because I kept a journal.

It was about all I had to fill my time, since I spent most of it sitting in the royal chambers, twiddling my thumbs while the ministers and other important people (as in, everyone except me) got on with ruling and taxing and whatever it was they told me not to worry my pretty little head about.

It was ninety-seven days since they came for me, ninety-four since they stuck the crown on that pretty little head.

I suppose that Gary of Ninety-Four Days didn't have quite the same ring to it.

Drusan was nothing if not careful about how things were presented.

I risked changing my position. I pushed some weight into my arms, lifted an elbow a couple of inches, and peeked back and under my arm to get a straight shot through into the other room.

Yep.

Drusan was on the throne.

I mean, he could have *asked* if he'd wanted it. I'd have surrendered it more than willingly. I hadn't even wanted to rule in the first place. He didn't have to stab me.

The hell of it was, he looked like he belonged.

Drusan was tall, willowy, and graceful. He had silky, dark blond hair in perfect ringlets that cascaded down the back of his very royal purple velvet frock coat. His cravat was always perfectly tied. The froth of lace at his wrists from beneath deep, folded-back cuffs was always flawlessly white. His long-fingered, artistic hands glittered with rings—pale, soft hands without even a hint of such common things as ink stains or pen calluses to mar them. Certainly no crooked bits from where he broke his little finger as a five-year-old.

He looked like he was born to rule. Perhaps he was. I'd heard rumours that his mother had elven blood and his father was descended from the old kings, a line that supposedly ended centuries ago.

Whether it was true or not, Drusan clearly felt at home.

He was draped over the carved and golden throne at his ease, one leg carelessly flung over the ornate arm.

You'd never tell by looking at him that he'd just stabbed a man in the back.

Literally.

I was on my way out of the council chamber when he did it, aware of someone close behind me but not paying any particular attention.

The huge room had been filled to capacity with courtiers, ministers, advisers, counsellors, and secretaries. I might have been king, but I wasn't fooling myself. I was the least important person there.

The meeting had finished and people were milling around, continuing their arguments about taxes, or troop movement plans, or trade embargoes, or whatever they'd been talking about. Even before I became king, I hadn't been remotely interested in politics.

They'd dressed me in the usual royal getup that morning—which I loathed— including the ridiculous satin slippers with large silver buckles and fashionable small red heels that I'd never got used to. They were too large for me. By then, the kingdom had gone through six kings in about nine months and, according to the head valet, the Exchequer couldn't afford to keep buying new outfits for kings who couldn't manage to stay alive.

He'd had a sneer on his face as he said it.

I think I was supposed to be offended.

I was too busy being owl-eyed and alarmed at the spill of silk and brocade finery spread out before me as they sorted through the dead kings' effects to find things that fit.

Unlike clothes, which you could cut down to size, you couldn't force shoes to fit.

The valet had one of his underlings haul in an enormous chest full of shoes for them to try on me, one after the other.

I had to sit on an uncomfortable gold chair while they dug through the pile and slipped shoe after shoe onto my stockinged foot. I was smaller than any of the others, the valet had snapped, as if my below-average height was a choice I'd made on purpose to inconvenience him. His clawed grip dug into my ankle more and more as he failed to find a decent pair.

All the while, I kept staring over his shoulder at the box. Trying hard not to see dead feet.

I was unsuccessful.

As luck would have it, the pair that I ended up with had previously belonged to my brother Gower. The valet told me this with great delight.

It was only in the last few years that the family fortunes had taken a turn for the better, and I'd been wearing Gower's cast-offs for most of my life.

I'd calmly told the man that stuffing the toes with a handkerchief per shoe would suffice.

I'd cried for Gower that night. And for my other brothers, Florian and Embray. Then I went all in and cried for the other kings who I was apparently related to but had never known. The lords of Silverleigh were, after all, the very last branch on the royal family tree.

Which made me the final, quivering twig.

It was down to Gower's shoes that I didn't die. I like to think that would make him smile.

Not quite as much as if I'd snatched the knife off Drusan and avenged his death. But close.

Even though I'd been used to wearing Gower's cast-offs, it didn't mean I could walk in them.

The toe of the overlong shoe caught in a crack between the flagstones and I hiccupped forward. My upper body folded about an inch as I shifted to regain my balance, and then I felt it.

A long, glancing scrape to the left of my spine, and a hard shove between my shoulder blades.

Puzzled at the sting, I twisted my hand back to investigate. When I held it up in front of my face, it was smeared with blood.

I...didn't do well with blood. Especially surprise blood.

I looked from the bright shine of red on my hand to Drusan's malicious smile, my eyes rolled up, and that was it.

I'd fainted.

Like a goat.

Now, keeping my eyes on the party in the throne room, ready to freeze before anyone saw me moving, I cautiously reached around and probed the area. I was wearing a stupid thick kingly robe over a heavy brocade frock coat. Beneath that, a quilted waistcoat. Beneath that, a shirt.

I felt the edges of the torn cloth but it was cool and sticky, not hot and wet. The blood wasn't flowing.

That had to be a good sign?

Bringing my hand back, I swallowed manfully and

braced myself for the sight of blood again—if I was prepared for it, maybe I wouldn't faint—and all I did was say a quiet, "Huh."

I'd already been moving away from Drusan's knife before he hit me with it. That, coupled with the accidental protection of all those ridiculous layers, meant that instead of delivering a death-dealing, kingdom-liberating stab, he'd managed to give me a wicked graze.

I'd had worse nosebleeds.

Which, yes. I'd also fainted at.

But still. It was a graze.

The traitor thought he'd killed me.

And he'd *smiled*.

I closed my eyes and held my breath as I heard the rapid patter of approaching footsteps.

The steps drew level with my motionless body, and bustled past.

I slitted my eyes open and watched as three servants laden down with trays of crystal glasses and canapés rushed the long length of the council chamber toward the throne room.

I caught another brief glance of the revelry orbiting Drusan before the broad backs of the servants blocked the view.

This was my moment.

I slipped my feet out of Gower's too-big shoes and eased my shoulders free of the heavy robe. Rolling up to my knees, I took a second to push the robe into a small mound of spilled purple and crimson, and hoped that a casual observer wouldn't notice that the robe was *sans* king. At least until I was clear.

I popped up to my feet, and legged it.

Where the goats had their survival strategy of fainting, I had one of my own that had served me well for years.

I had a long and successful history of running.

I was grateful that my attempted murder had happened at this end of the chamber, because it opened onto the private residence and servants area, meaning I didn't have to flee under the noses of the Royal Guard, who would have stopped me. And probably given the stabbing a second go.

Since they were guards not courtiers, they would have done a better job of it than Drusan.

And they also had big pikes, rather than sneaky little daggers.

Like the one that Drusan must have had on his person, maybe up his sleeve, the whole morning he sat beside me and smiled and murmured in my ear.

The bastard.

I'd trusted him. Foolishly, yes. But I had. I didn't think I would ever trust anyone again.

Halfway down the Long Gallery, I ducked into a deeply recessed window embrasure and attempted to become one with the shadows as a clot of braying courtiers hustled past. Heading for the party, no doubt.

Word was spreading.

They didn't notice me.

I ducked back out and made it to the small door at the far end. I darted through the quiet servants' passageway to another door at the far end of that. It opened onto a long spiralling staircase in one of the lesser-used towers.

I whisked down the worn-smooth steps, trailing one hand along the wall to keep my balance. I strained my ears for any sound of pursuit, but all I heard was the noise of my stockinged feet pattering over stone, and the thundering of my panicked heart.

I jumped the last three steps, hurled myself at the small postern, and exploded out onto a gravel path.

Ow.

The gravel was small and sharp, and bit into the soles of my feet. I scrambled off the path and onto the lawn as quickly as I could, and hared off.

If I was a smarter man, I'd have taken a detour to my chambers, grabbed some essentials and a weapon or two, and then made my escape with an actual direction in mind.

Or a plan.

A plan. Yes. I'd get right on that, just as soon as I had a moment to catch my breath.

I skirted the Pleasure Gardens, ran along the tall yew hedges of one of the Palace's famed mazes, and found my way to the less visually appealing but infinitely more useful area of the grounds; the vegetable gardens.

It had been raining since the day before yesterday. While gardeners didn't get to take the day off just because of poor weather, they did tend to stick to the greenhouses or potting sheds when it was really coming down. I had managed to escape the Palace unseen.

I intended to escape the grounds the same way.

It was a risk, but by the time I'd run far enough that I'd made it to the outskirts of even the functional gardens, I knew that I had to at least poke my nose into one of the sheds. I was growing damper by the minute. My stockings were already soaked through and filthy.

I wouldn't get far without boots, and without a coat at this time of year, I'd freeze to death.

I kept running, until I spotted a likely shed.

It was a small and ramshackle structure with a distinct lean, and moss on the roof. I guessed it was used for tool storage, or perhaps was no longer in use at all, considering its dilapidated state.

I dashed up to it and sidled along with my back to the wall until I could duck my head and peer in through a cobwebbed window.

It was empty.

Gasping with relief, I shot around the side, yanked the door open, and darted in, closing the door behind me.

Rain pattered on the wooden roof and whispered over the grimy window pane.

I'd been right in my guess that it was probably used for tool storage—a jumble of rakes and spades and forks were propped up against the far wall, and every shelf was stuffed with broken pots and battered tubs.

I'd been wrong in my guess that it wasn't in use, though.

The long potting bench had a scattering of fresh dirt and some potted-up seedlings lined along it. Earthenware mugs and plates clustered at one end.

The oil lamp, when I reached out and touched the glass shade, held a faint trace of warmth.

Whoever had gone was gone recently, and could very well be back.

Shit.

I'd been hoping to take a breath, but it seemed my luck was running out.

Not completely, however.

A rack of worn-out coats and a mess of boots stood inside by the door. Feeling guilty even though I doubted anyone would notice anything was missing, let alone be angry about it, I rooted through the garments until I found the largest, bulkiest one I could find.

I pulled it off the peg with a subdued crow of triumph.

The ankle-length greatcoat was stained and patched, it

smelled like mildew, and I didn't want to put my hands in the pockets in case I found a mouse or a spider.

I was wet, shuddering with cold, and on the run.

I couldn't get into it quickly enough.

I shrugged it on as eagerly as I'd shrugged off my kingly robes, and dragged it around me. It was clammy and fairly disgusting, but it was made of thick wool and would offer some protection for the road.

Thinking of the robes made me think of the throne room. Had anyone noticed I was gone yet? Would they be scouring the Palace, looking for me?

I'd taken too long.

I pawed through the boots until I found a pair likely to be my size. I tried them on, and kicked them back off at once. They were ridiculously large. I scuffed around and came up with another pair. Much too large again, but marginally less so. At that point, I wasn't in a position to linger. I shoved them on and called it good.

Cracking the door open, I peered out. When all I saw was a grey curtain of mizzling rain, I slid out and shut the door behind me.

Half an hour ago—or more, depending on how long I'd lain unconscious on the council chamber floor—I'd been a king in robes.

And now I was a fugitive in rags.

I wasn't what you'd call *happy* about the fugitive or the rags bit.

But I was thrilled to no longer be king.

Ducking my head against the rain, I set off into the darkening day.

2

My journey into the capital city was a very, very different experience from my journey out.

Then, I rode in a carriage filled with satin pillows, boxes of bonbons which I did not eat, crystal glasses of sparkling wine which I did not drink, and overly friendly ministers with murder on their minds.

I hadn't suspected a thing.

People had lined the cobbled streets of Jarra, waving handkerchiefs and bright little flags, cheering politely as I passed.

I'd huddled in a corner of the carriage until Drusan dragged me to the window and instructed me to smile, and wave back. I was their saviour, wasn't I? Bringing peace and stability after a decade of turmoil and, in this last year alone, a run of six bad kings who had made it to the crown, and another five pretenders besides? Let the people see me and rejoice!

How was I supposed to bring peace and stability? I'd

demanded in a panicked whisper. I didn't know how to rule. I didn't know how to navigate Court. I could barely navigate afternoon tea. I'd lived my whole life five hundred miles away on the northernmost estate in the kingdom. I didn't know any of this had been happening!

I certainly hadn't known my older brothers had each tried their hand at being king.

Since my father had died before the line of succession narrowed in on our family, Florian, as the current Lord of Silverleigh, was the first.

He'd made it to Jarra from his summer estate in the south, but he hadn't lasted long enough for his coronation.

Embray was killed by bandits on the road here.

Gower had ruled for two weeks.

Then he was decapitated in bed, a team effort from the man and the woman he'd retired with for the night.

Leave it all to me, Drusan had replied, patting my hand. I know exactly what to do.

The carriage had processed through the city along a wide, paved road, with Drusan pointing out various landmarks and places of interest as we went. I was too overwhelmed by the sheer noise and press of people to pay attention.

He made sure that I was looking when we drove past the enormous public square with blackened flagstones at the centre.

That, Drusan had said, pulling a sad face, was where they held the kings' funeral pyres. No amount of scrubbing seemed to get the soot stains out. It was baked in, apparently. A royal pyre had to burn hot and beautiful to burn a king to ash.

I'd gaped at him.

He'd patted my hand again, and told me to trust him and

I'd be fine, then looked appalled and passed me a lace-trimmed handkerchief when my eyes had started to leak.

They wouldn't be burning *this* king to ash, I thought grimly as I made my way through the city in a shabby greatcoat and stolen boots.

For one thing, good luck lighting a pyre in this weather, even with a barrel of oil.

For another, I didn't plan on sticking around.

It was hard to believe that I had clung onto the throne for the longest in two years, avoiding death by assassination over and over again. I'd never considered myself a lucky person, but at times it seemed almost as if someone was watching over me.

Jarra was loud and crowded, and humid. Carriages and carts choked the roads and people thronged the pavements, all yelling and jostling and shoving.

The rain continued.

It had plastered my hair flat and turned my pale blond to dull brown. My scalp tingled with cold. Chill rain dripped off my nose and slithered down the back of my collar, even though I'd turned it up and hunkered in, attempting to shield my face not just from the rain but from passersby.

My heart pounded, blood rushing in my ears. I was terrified that someone would stop, point, and shout, *The King! The Tyrant King! Get him!*

Nobody noticed me, of course. Why would they? I was swathed up to the eyebrows in a cheap greatcoat, like most of the other people on the streets.

I'd exited the back of the Palace gardens through a tiny wicket gate in a hedge which had spat me out in a rough area of the city, filled with taverns and shops and street markets. I fit right in.

And then there were all the posters, pasted up in shop

windows and pinned to noticeboards and doorways. I only gave them a second look because they were everywhere. Someone must have spent a fortune printing and distributing them.

They were extremely unflattering.

They all showed a haughty and arrogant face with large, ice-pale eyes, sharp cheekbones, a pointed chin, and a sinister sneer.

The hair colour was the only thing they'd got right, although they'd drawn it in a charming drift of chin-length silvery blond.

It was an incongruously kind way to depict my unruly mop, I thought. On my best day, I had hair like a dandelion clock.

I didn't even realise it was supposed to be me until I read my name beneath the portrait, along with various explicit suggestions as to what, exactly, I could do with my royal sceptre (I had a sceptre?) and where I could get off taxing the poor again (I taxed people?) and how I was a warmonger who would never be satisfied and had sent our youth to their deaths (I'd sent who where?).

I'd have to check my journals, because I could be scatty from time to time, it was true, but I was pretty sure I hadn't *sent anyone off to war.*

What else had Drusan done in my name? I shuddered to think.

As soon as possible, I slipped down a side alley, and then another, and then another, until the boisterous hustle of the main thoroughfare was a faint hum and the loudest sound was the hiss of rain and the gurgling gutters.

It occurred to me that I could wander lost in the maze-like city for days.

I didn't know if the guards would start—or were already

in the process of—combing the streets for me, or if Drusan had even noticed I was gone.

Were there rumours of my demise yet? Or had Drusan shrugged his shoulders when I was discovered missing, and thought, it doesn't matter.

Since he was the Liberator.

Dead or alive, I'd been dethroned.

I continued on, jog-walking briskly when there were people around, and flat-out running when there weren't. I'd seen the old city walls in the hazy distance whenever someone made me go out onto the Public Balcony at the Palace. As long as I managed to keep heading in the same direction, I hoped that I'd eventually reach the edge of the city.

The Palace was on high ground, and the approach was along a straight road, similar to the long drive up to Silverleigh but on a much grander scale.

The original castle keep had been expanded and added to until it became a palace. The settlement that had grown up around the keep went from village to town, and then the town expanded into a city.

I cobbled together a simple plan as I wove through the unfamiliar streets.

There were six gates in the walls. Six ways out that didn't require a grappling hook or a ladder.

First, I would find the wall. Then I'd follow along it, like a mouse running along the skirting board, until I found one of the gates.

After that, all I had to do was get past the guards, and run like hell for home.

It was a rough plan, full of hope and holes, and probably doomed to fail, but what other choice did I have?

One thing was going right, at least: there was no hue and cry, and no sign that I was being pursued.

The worst moment came when I'd made it to the gate. It was around mid-morning by then, and the traffic in and out was light. I guessed it was busiest at the start and end of the day.

Of the six gates, I'd managed to find the one in the worst district. The buildings were old, run-down, and shabby. I lurked in the shadows cast by a drunkenly leaning house with an upper storey that jutted out so far over the narrow street that it almost touched the equally perilous overhang of the building across the way.

I watched and waited.

It was definitely going to be easier to get out of this gate unnoticed than if I'd tried to stroll out the main gates.

The massive wrought iron ones that my carriage had bowled in through were a work of art, with curlicues, javelin-sharp golden tips, and a few centuries' worth of pomp and ceremony behind them.

This one was little more than a rusted grille set beside a crumbling guardhouse at the back end of the slums.

There were only two guards, and neither of them were particularly sharp-looking.

Their uniforms were plain, all they seemed to do was have a natter with anyone coming in or out, and apart from yelling now and then at passing groups of urchins, who'd yell back twice as loud, that was all they did.

I hovered as long as I could without being conspicuous, waiting for the right moment. When a large cart rumbled past, laden with sacks and barrels, I made my move.

Shoving my hands in my pockets and hunkering deep within the folds of my stolen coat, I strode after it on shaky legs.

Focused intently on the gate while also trying to give the vague impression that I was with the cart, I didn't notice that the cart had slowed and stopped as the driver chatted to one of the guards.

I oofed right into it.

The waist-high bed caught me square in the middle, air shot out of me in a high whistle, and I braced my hands on the tailgate to stop myself from slipping in the mud.

The collar I'd been gripping high at my throat flopped down to reveal my face.

Right as I caught the attention of the other guard.

I froze.

No! Don't freeze! Don't be suspicious!

I'd watched enough people go in and out to have picked up that a simple nod of acknowledgement would suffice.

I tipped my chin, thought, *Oh my gods that's way too regal*, attempted to adjust from a haughty nod to a friendly hello, and ended up making a strange little head wobble at the guard.

His eyes widened slightly.

I went red, flipped the collar back up, tucked my chin, and strode on.

He didn't stop me.

I managed to stay at a brisk yet unsuspicious pace and not break out into a sprint.

When I chanced a look back, the cart was on the move, rolling sedately behind me. One guard was picking his teeth. The other had called over one of the street boys and was deep in conversation with him.

Neither were looking my way.

The houses spilling out from the city thinned and thinned until there were no buildings left at all. The cart overtook me. It turned off the main road. A handful more carts rumbled past, a couple of lone riders splashed me with muddy water as they cantered by, but eventually there were fewer and fewer places to turn off, and it was just a long straight road ahead.

Straight didn't mean easy.

This far out from the capital, the road was like any around home. Wide enough for two carriages to pass, but nothing special in the way of surfacing.

In other words, it was pitted with ruts and puddles that made for uncomfortable walking, and much tripping and twisting of ankles.

I'd been trudging along for hours by the time I realised that the gloom wasn't due to the rain anymore. In fact, it had mostly stopped raining.

I glanced up at the sky. A waxing moon was half-hidden behind a bank of ragged clouds.

Ah, yes. Night. Forgot about that.

Wonderful.

The further I went, the thicker the vegetation either side grew. Low shrubs became medium-sized shrubs became small trees, until soon there was no hiding from it.

I was very much in the woods at this point.

Not the deep dark woods where you'd find bandit camps, trolls, ancient gods and the like.

But...fair chance of bears, I'd say.

My shoulders were already tight and hunched from the cold as I jog-walked along as best I could in my overlarge boots, arms wrapped around my middle and head down against the occasional gust of rain.

As soon as I thought of bears, thoughts of wolves came along.

My shoulders crawled all the way up to my ears.

I wished it was simply the possibility of wild animals that was making me jumpy. It wasn't.

It was certainty.

Bone-deep, skin-prickling, bowel-loosening certainty. Something was already following me.

Or...someone?

I couldn't decide which was worse.

Bear, assassin, betrayer—whoever or whatever was following me, I did not want them to catch up. I stepped up my jog-walk to a proper jog, or at least the best I could manage.

I was tired and stumbling. I was frozen. My feet were numb. And a small part of me was saying, *Why are you running, Gary? You know you're not getting out of this. You've been marked for death. Embrace your destiny.*

The rest of me said, *No. I will not.*

I set my jaw and pushed harder, spraying up water from the rutted road, my arms flying out every now and then as I struggled to keep my balance.

I was not going to trip again, dammit.

And then I heard a noise.

It was a deep...bellow? Or a roar, or...?

I didn't know.

I couldn't hear much of anything over the rush of blood in my ears, accompanied by a strange, high-pitched ringing.

This is what true fear sounds like, I thought hysterically.

I hadn't even been this afraid when it dawned on me that Drusan had literally stabbed me in the back.

Because Drusan had just wanted me dead. He wouldn't have eaten me afterward.

Gods, I didn't want to be eaten.

I *refused*.

I picked up the pace into a flat-out sprint. It was an ungainly, shambling run; legs pumping, arms too, trying to force myself along using willpower where my exhausted body was failing.

All too soon, I reached the point where I couldn't run any longer.

With the best will in the world—and I was so, so very motivated to not be dinner—I couldn't drag my leaden limbs any further. I stumbled once, twice, staggered to a defeated halt, and crashed to my knees.

Head bowed, I closed my eyes and waited for whatever was chasing me to spring upon my defenceless body.

Nothing happened.

Nothing...continued to happen.

The ringing in my ears faded. I still heard my ragged breathing, and my over-fast heartbeat drummed at my skin from within, but it was slowly, ridiculously, calming.

I straightened and stared down the long, dark road that lay behind me. Now that the rain had stopped and the moon was out, visibility was excellent.

The road was completely empty, save for puddles and ruts.

I got all the way to my feet and turned to face the empty road. Putting my hands on my hips, I broke into a smile.

I'd outrun it.

I slumped with relief.

I was cheating death left, right and centre at this point, wasn't I? I'd never really thought of myself as the canny survivor type before.

Perhaps I should start?

They were calling me terrible things in Jarra. I'd heard more than a few as I slunk through the bustling streets.

Instead of all those awful names, I decided, they should call me Gary, the Survivor.

Or Gary, Outrunner of Bears.

Ooh. Gary, the Uncatchable.

A twig cracked behind me.

Every muscle in my tired, aching body locked and my smile vanished. I hadn't outrun anything.

It had circled around me, hadn't it? It had got ahead, and was coming up behind me.

Gary, the Overly Optimistic.

I pressed my lips together to hold in a whimper.

This was too cruel. It was too much.

Thuds on the road. A shifting rock. The squelch of heavy, purposeful steps, drawing inexorably closer. They stopped some distance away.

I braced myself.

Here comes the snarling, explosive launch across the distance.

"My lord," someone said.

A whimper of fear broke out despite my best efforts.

It wasn't a bear or a wolf, at least. Because bears or wolves didn't usually address you by your title.

Unless they were enchanted.

And even that was an improvement, because then at least there was a chance, wasn't there, of talking them out of it?

I puffed out three short breaths like I was preparing myself to dive into the lake at home, put my shoulders back, and turned to face my pursuer.

He stood there, waiting, a good twenty feet away. A tall, broad shape in the darkness that was oddly familiar. I squinted but I couldn't quite—

"My lord," the enchanted bear/troll/bandit said again, in a deep voice with a northern accent that I knew.

I *knew* it.

And that was the biggest shock of all, the sound of *his* voice here where I genuinely thought I was more likely to come across a talking bear than him.

"Magnus!" I flew across the distance between us.

As soon as I moved, he did too. We crashed together.

He didn't even sway as I bounced off him and then scrambled back, closer, throwing my arms around him.

Was this an inappropriate way for a lord to greet his stable master?

Very much yes.

I didn't care. It was all I could do not to start climbing him.

Magnus.

Magnus was *here*.

I locked my arms around his sturdy, solid body and panted into his chest, the rough fabric of his greatcoat scratching my face. He tipped his head down and rested his chin on the top of my head for a moment, his arms tight around me, and squeezing tighter.

He was squeezing a bit too hard, actually.

I didn't mind it. He was so warm. I'd been so cold for so long.

I had been cold since they took me away from him.

From Silverleigh, I mean.

He murmured something into my damp hair. I couldn't catch the words but it sounded heartfelt. His chest beneath my cheek expanded in a deep, deep breath. When he let it out, he curved over me. He straightened, lifting me off my feet, and held me tighter.

My jangling heart and hectic breaths slowed and evened out as he held me. I was completely enveloped by him.

I kept my eyes closed tight and let his warmth, his scent, soak into me.

Magnus smelled like home.

Like sunshine on freshly cut hay, like the stables and the herb garden, and everything I'd missed with every passing second since they put me in the carriage.

I took in deep lungfuls of it, hoping that it wasn't too obvious. I must have been a dead weight, but his arms didn't even quiver.

Eventually, though, I had to let go.

...did I?

Yes. Yes, I did. This really wasn't appropriate.

But my relief that he wasn't a bear, or Drusan come to finish the job, or a random traveler who loathed me because of all the things that were done in my name, was short-lived.

As his delicious, soothing scent and warmth soaked into me and calmed my frantic, scurrying thoughts, it left room for doubt to creep in.

What, exactly, was Magnus doing here?

He was my stable master.

Ergo, he should be in my stables, hundreds and hundreds of miles away.

But he just so happened to be here.

On a random road, in the dark and the rain.

At the exact same time as I was here.

All of the muscles that had softened with relief as he held me in his arms locked tight.

No. Gods, no.

Not Magnus, too. It was one thing for Drusan or anyone from the Palace to do it. If Magnus shivved me, I'd die.

Of a broken heart, probably, since against all odds I seemed to have a knack for avoiding death by blades.

But I would *die*.

Magnus made a surprised noise when I went rigid. He set me down carefully. The whole time, I was expecting a bright glance of deadly sensation to find its way through my ribs.

The instant my boots hit the road, I ran.

3

I got about ten steps before I tripped and went down to hands and knees.

Shit.

I scrambled up, but it was too late. Magnus was upon me.

He grabbed me around the waist, hauled me up, and...set me back on my feet.

I scraped my sodden mop of hair away from my face, took a breath, then started slapping at his hands and kicking wildly.

Magnus held me by the front of the greatcoat, pushed me back a step, and locked his elbow, keeping me at arm's length.

I landed a couple of glancing kicks against his shins but his reach was much longer than mine. I couldn't get at any part of him other than the hand in my coat.

I started trying to bend his fingers back.

Of course, Magnus was used to wrangling stroppy great stallions who had over a thousand pounds more muscle behind their temper tantrums than I did. If he could control them without breaking a sweat, what possible challenge could I offer?

Still, I gave it my best shot.

Magnus' brows rose as he watched me flail, a deeply unimpressed expression on his hawkish face.

"Are you done?" he said eventually.

"No!" I squirmed. "*Hhhhnnn.*"

"My lord," he said on an exasperated sigh.

I writhed.

Magnus tugged, reeling me in until I collided with his body. He cupped my face and tipped his head down to look directly into my eyes. "Gary," he said softly.

I stopped squirming. My hands came up and curled around his powerful wrists. His bare skin was hot against my cold, clammy fingers. I gasped. "Magnus. Please don't try to kill me too."

He brushed my hair back and tucked it behind my ears. "I'm a little offended that you'd even say such a thing. Why would I ever want to kill you?"

I blinked. "I don't *know*! Everyone else in the whole world seems to want me dead. Including Drusan, who, up until this morning, I thought was my only friend. Why not you, too? Why else would you be here, if not to kill me?" I dropped my hands from his wrists with the intention of shoving at him, but all I did was grab onto his hard waist.

"You can't think of any other reason? One more likely than I suddenly, after six years at Silverleigh, decided to cross the kingdom on a whim to find you and kill you? Or am I an assassin in my spare time? Is that what it is?"

I stared up at him.

His nostrils flared. "You can't think of any other reason, Gary?"

It sank in that he wasn't calling me m'lord.

Until recently, people very rarely said my name.

This morning, as I lay on the council chamber floor, and then as I passed through the city, I'd heard it more than I cared for. It was attached to such delightful phrases as, *Huzzah, Gary is dead*. And, *Down with Gary*. And, *Death to Gary, the Tyrant King*.

My father called me Boy. My brothers called me Oi, and You, and You Fucking Idiot, and Little Brother.

The servants called me my lord.

In fact, since my mother died when I was eight, I very rarely ever heard my name. There was simply no one around to use it.

While yes, I may have daydreamed on occasion what my name would sound like in Magnus' deep voice, I hadn't ever actually expected to hear him say it.

"Gary," he said again, and I shivered. "Why do you think I'm here?"

"Um. You brought Hazlette?"

It was the only reason I could think of. Hazlette was my horse, Magnus had bought her especially for me, and she was the only horse in the stable he would ever let me get on, because I had a terrible habit of falling off. He was absolutely fanatical about it.

It was one of his *rules*, and when it came to his rules?

Magnus Torlassen did not bend.

"No, Gary. I didn't travel five hundred miles and then hang around in the city for three months to bring your horse, either." He stroked his thumb along my jaw as his gaze roamed over my face. "Would you like another guess?"

"Are you here to help me?"

"Someone has to."

I grimaced. "But how did you even know to find me

here?" Looking around, I gestured wildly. "You popped up out of nowhere."

He snorted. "I arrived in Jarra a day after you."

When Drusan, his retinue, and a platoon of royal guards had put me in the carriage, some of the servants had put up a fuss. Mostly because *I'd* put up a fuss. I'd said no. Loudly. Also repeatedly.

Drusan hadn't listened.

I'd heard a scuffle outside the carriage, some shouting—I'd recognised Magnus' voice, and some of the lads'. Mrs Robards' wrathful screeching, too—and the clashing of steel, but it hadn't lasted long.

I'd assumed, somewhat dolefully, that once I'd left, they'd all gone back to their daily routine.

I'd never thought that anyone would come after me.

"You've been here the whole time?" I wish I'd known. I wouldn't have felt so staggeringly lost and lonely.

"I was on the road behind you not two hours after they took you," he said.

I gripped his sleeves. "But why?"

He tilted his head, narrowing his eyes. "Why do you think?"

There was something both teasing and fierce in his expression that made me glance away.

"I came for *you*, Gary. How the hell were you ever going to survive as king, when kings these days have the life expectancy of a mayfly?"

"I wasn't supposed to," I told him. "That was the whole point." It was also where my understanding of the political situation started and ended.

"If I'd known a few months ago you were even close to the line of succession, I'd already have taken you away," Magnus said.

"Why didn't you tell me you were in the city? What have you been *doing*? Magnus, you could have come to see me, or sent me a note. Or something!"

"I tried. They had you locked up tight. I couldn't even get taken on in the stables. *Me*." He sounded faintly indignant at that. "I couldn't get close myself, but it was easy enough to bribe the people who could. Funny thing about corruption. Loyalty is for sale, and the highest bidder wins. You probably think it's just Drusan after the crown."

I hated to expose my ignorance here, but I had no idea what was going on, other than everyone hated me.

It was ridiculous.

I was nominally the king, I'd just been 'assassinated', and I remained clueless, beyond: political turmoil is happening.

I made a vaguely agreeing noise.

"Well, it wasn't just Drusan," Magnus said. "That city is a seething cauldron of backstabbing, wheeling-dealing, promise-making and promise-breaking, alliance-shifting bullshit. Surprisingly enough, not everyone wanted you dead. Quite a few people wanted you alive."

I blinked. "That's nice?"

"At least three rival factions wanted to keep you on as a puppet."

"Oh." Not so nice.

"Two Estlan dukes wanted to marry you to their daughters, get an heir out of you and then kill you."

"Ah—"

"A marchioness had a plan to make it past the guards to your solitary confinement and have you knock her up and claim the throne by regency for her heir."

My eyes bulged. *Have* me knock her up?

Wait. Solitary confinement?

"I didn't care for that one," Magnus said coldly.

I'd been in solitary confinement?

"The Valdrani ambassador was caught scheming to kidnap you, transport you to Valdran, and claim an engagement from the cradle between you and the Crown Prince. And I could tell you more, but we have more important things to be doing than standing around discussing it."

"Yes, of course. We should get off the road. I'm probably the most wanted man in the kingdom right now, aren't I?" If, that was, anyone had stopped toasting my death long enough to notice that the dead body had got up and wandered off.

Have fun explaining that one, Drusan.

Magnus made a show of looking around the dark, deserted road with the louring woods on either side. "I think we're safe. Besides, as far as the general populace is concerned, you're already dead."

I squawked when Magnus snatched me to him.

"I thought..." He shook his head and tugged me closer. "Gods. I thought..."

He was breathing hard. At a loss, I patted his back awkwardly. "There, there."

For some reason, this made him laugh. He released me, running his sharp gaze over me again.

"I'm all right," I told him. My Wound of Betrayal wasn't even throbbing. The blisters on my heels were worse.

"Thank the fucking gods. Gary. I thought I'd lost you."

"Oh. Well, I'm—*eep*." He yanked me in again and pressed a hard kiss to the top of my head.

I was a bit flustered with all the attention. I can't lie, though. I was enjoying it.

"I honestly had no idea about any of this," I said. "Other than the short life-expectancy, of course."

I'd been sitting in my chamber, apparently in solitary confinement and entirely too stupid to know it, spending most of my days journaling.

I bet Drusan had been reading them the whole time. Perhaps for some light relief between plotting my death and taxing the poor.

I hoped he enjoyed all the mooning about Magnus, because that was mostly what filled the pages. Along with a lot of repetitive oh-gods-I'm-going-to-die panic.

"How do you know so much about all of this?" I asked Magnus.

"Because I made it my business to find out, Gary. I was bribing half the fucking city to keep me informed of your movements, Drusan's movements, Palace gossip. The works. I bribed servants, guards, street rats, society ladies, lords, clerks, ministers. I made sure that if anyone so much as whispered your name, I'd hear about it."

By the look on his face, he heard a lot, and none of it was nice.

"Are you a stable master or a spymaster?" I marvelled.

"Neither." He stroked my chin again. I tipped my head and leaned into it like a cat.

"Must have given you a fright when you heard about what happened in the council chamber this morning, then," I said, soaking up the warmth of his hand on my face.

Magnus stilled. "What did happen in the council chamber?"

Now I stilled.

We stared at each other.

"What?" I said.

"I didn't hear anything about the council chamber," he said.

"You didn't?"

"No."

"Then why are you here?" Was he psychic?

"A street rat found me in my lodgings with a message from a guard at the Northern gate who swore he watched you leave the city on foot. The guard's a dependable source. He works shifts up at the Palace and he's seen you before."

I *knew* the man had recognised me.

"When I was already on my way through the city to come after you," Magnus said, "I started hearing reports that you were dead and they were lighting the bonfire in an hour." He closed his eyes briefly. "By the time I was on the road, the celebrations had started. All I could do was push forward and hope that you'd escaped and I'd find you."

"That sounds very stressful."

"It was. What happened in the council chamber?"

I waved it off. "Oh. Nothing important. Bonfire, you said? You mean my pyre?"

He shook his head. "Definitely a bonfire. A pyre is for mourning. Tyrants get burned like last year's dead leaves. Especially tyrants whose bodies have disappeared when Drusan has already seized power. It was ramping up to quite the party by the time I left."

Magnus' words were light. His expression was haunted.

I still had my arms around him. I patted him again. "Whoever they're burning, it's not me," I said.

"Mm," he said. "Probably dug out the shortest guy in the dungeon, put a wig on him and dressed him in your robes. The chamber, Gary?"

He already seemed upset about the bonfire. I got the feeling that if I told him Drusan had actually stabbed me, Magnus would get *very* upset. I decided to hedge. "Honestly, nothing much. They tried to kill me again. You know. The usual. I, uh, played dead long enough to make them think they'd managed it this time. When no one was looking, I ran."

"You tricked them?"

Magnus looked so proud, I didn't have the heart to tell him that it hadn't been on purpose. I'd just fainted. "Yes?"

He grinned at me.

"Yes," I said, playing it off casually. As if my actions had been anything other than animal instinct. "I saw a moment to run, and I took it."

I was intimidated and embarrassed at the idea that while I'd been sitting around, twiddling my thumbs and journaling in solitary confinement like a fool, Magnus had been setting up a spy network and bribing everyone.

"Thank you for coming, Magnus. I don't know what I'd do without you here."

I'd got myself out of the Palace and Jarra, but over the last couple of hours it had begun to dawn on me that I was hardly out of peril.

Magnus lifted my chin. He squeezed, gentle but firm, and when he spoke, his words were slow and deliberate. "Of course I came for you, Gary. I will always come for you. Always. You're my—"

I gazed up into his dark chestnut eyes.

What?

I was his what?

We were plastered together, from knees to chest. My arms were locked around him.

He was holding my face.

Somehow, I didn't think he was going to finish that sentence with *my employer*.

"I'm your...?" I prompted.

He didn't reply.

Instead, Magnus leaned down and laid his lips gently to mine.

4

He held there for a long moment. This was my first kiss, and I wasn't quite sure what to do.

I *was* sure that I didn't want Magnus to know that the closest I'd ever got to kissing was seeing other people do it.

Unwittingly, I would like to add. I didn't lurk around hoping to catch people at it.

It wasn't something I particularly enjoyed witnessing. I hadn't even thought that it was something I'd like to try out for myself.

Except...

Over the past three years, since the day I'd fallen off Hazlette rather more dramatically than usual, and Magnus had carried me to my room while bellowing for the physician, I'd begun to wonder what it might be like to kiss him.

But only Magnus.

The other kisses I kept seeing had all been quite unnerving. It seemed to happen all the time. All over the estate. House *and* grounds. People were always doing it. Was that normal? I didn't know.

I caught the maids at it, Arne the estate manager and

Mrs Robards the housekeeper. The gardeners, the footmen, the stable lads. Guests, visitors, couriers.

In fact, if I sat down with one of my journals, wrote a list of all the people on the estate, and marked off whether or not I'd seen them kissing someone?

I estimated that at least sixty percent would have a check mark by their name.

From a purely observational standpoint, the whole business of kissing looked quite horrifying.

The first time I'd stumbled across it, I'd thought...well, I was ten years old. I couldn't begin to guess what was happening.

All I could think was that Elayne, one of the chambermaids, and Jafray, one of the gardeners, were engaged in some kind of hostile tussle, and things had devolved to biting.

It wasn't anything like the odd snatched buss on the cheek I'd seen every now and then, despite how sheltered my mother had kept me. I'd even had kisses on the cheek myself, from Mother and from any of her friends, back when she was still well enough to receive visitors.

But this, what was happening between Elayne and Jafray, this wasn't a light brush that barely landed before flitting off. Their faces were mashed together, and their jaws were moving.

I'd dithered anxiously, wondering whether or not I should intervene, when it dawned on me that they were sighing and giggling at the same time as they were wrestling. Elayne had wound her arms around Jafray's broad back and she kept pulling him closer, rather than smacking him and stalking off back to the kitchen.

Elayne didn't take any nonsense from anyone. If Jafray

was looming over her, then it was because she permitted it, or he'd know otherwise.

I had backed away without them being any the wiser.

I'd seen Magnus kissing lots of people.

Make that men. I'd never seen Magnus kissing a woman, even though they sighed and fluttered around him often enough, and he clearly appreciated their company.

When Magnus kissed someone, it didn't look awful.

Sometimes Magnus had held the lads for it. Usually it was a stable lad. Sometimes a courier, or a visiting land agent or horse breeder. He'd hold them steady between his big, firm hands, or push them up against the wall.

Sometimes he hadn't held them at all. It was nothing more than a laughing, hearty kiss dropped on their eager mouths as he passed them by. They nearly always tried to get more.

One way or the other, the feeling stirred in me when I saw Magnus kissing someone wasn't the usual faint horror.

It was worse.

It was faint curiosity.

I hadn't allowed myself to indulge in too many daydreams about Magnus and kissing. There was little point. I had a wonderful imagination, but I never quite managed to see myself in the role as the sort of tempting young man Magnus might want to spend an afternoon with.

Once or twice I'd closed my eyes and thought about it.

But nothing had prepared me for this.

Magnus either didn't notice my frozen cluelessness or he didn't mind it.

He lifted his head after a warm press of our mouths together. It hadn't lasted long. He smiled down at me, his tanned cheeks dusky under his pepper-and-salt stubble, and his beautiful eyes bright.

He was *lovely*.

I wanted to kiss him again.

I swayed awkwardly toward him. Unfortunately, Magnus caught me and straightened me up. He took my hand in a firm grip and set off, pausing to grab the strap of a large pack he must have dropped when I threw myself at him earlier. He hitched it up over his shoulder and confidently marched us clean off the road, into the tree line and beyond.

I plastered myself to his side.

I was a great admirer of nature. My preference was to admire it in the enormous books with beautiful illustrated plates in my library, and with a nice cup of tea.

Maybe a scone.

It took at least three minutes before I regained my wits enough to ask, "Where are we going? Do you know where we're going? This is a much thicker wood than the one at home. Thickest I've ever been in, actually. There are lots more trees. Are there bears?"

I should have been asking other questions, such as: what on earth did Magnus think he was doing, addressing me by my given name, and why was he suddenly kissing me like I was one of the stable lads?

Neither of these seemed important.

Certainly less important than the possibility of hungry wildlife.

And I'd been thrilled by both actions and very much hoped he'd do them again. I'd hate to put him off.

"Yes, I know where we're going," Magnus said. "Yes, there are a lot of trees. You get that in a forest, which is what we're in. Not a wood. Technically, it's not just a forest, it's the King's Chase, with all timber and hunting rights owned by the crown. You own it."

I looked around, bewildered. "I do?"

"Yes, you do. And yes to bears. Which you also own."

He laughed when I immediately tried to get closer. Short of mounting him, it was impossible. But I tried.

Weak moonlight filtered through the canopy of dark, heavy branches; it gleamed off Magnus' smile and his eyes. "I'll protect you," he said.

"Thank you. How kind. And while you are fairly terrifying, Magnus, you're probably not all that terrifying to a bear? So I think we should go back out onto the road?"

"Bears can also use roads. We're fine." He was quiet for a second. "Fairly terrifying? You're not afraid of me, are you?"

"Pfft," I said and flapped a hand. Magnus' tension eased, until I blithely continued, "Of course I am."

"What?"

I shrugged and nodded. "You're a big man," I said. "You could snap me like a twig."

Magnus frowned. "I can be gentle," he chided.

"Oh, I know that. I've seen you with the horses. And with the—" *stable lads*, I nearly said, but cut myself off in time.

Or not.

Magnus glanced at me. "And with the..?" he prompted.

"Um." *Think*, Gary. "The, um..."

Magnus kept looking at me.

"Kittens," I said. "I have seen you in the stables. With the stable kittens."

I had never once seen Magnus with kittens.

But there were plenty of cats in the sprawling stable block, for the purpose of mouse control. I myself had spent many a long, contented day playing with their kittens in the hayloft. They were adorable.

Nobody could resist kittens.

Except, apparently, Magnus.

"Cats make me sneeze," Magnus said. "I stay far away

from them." He considered me and began to smile. It was a slow, wicked thing. "Did you see me with a lad every now and then, Gary?"

I could deny it. But why bother? "Yes, with a lad now and then." And he hadn't necessarily been gentle with them, but, "They always seemed to be having a good time."

"I aim to please."

"At first I thought you were, um, disciplining them, what with all the noise they made. But they left smiling, so. I suppose not."

Magnus stopped and stared down at me.

Thank goodness it was dark.

I could barely see a thing, which meant that Magnus couldn't either. It was a relief—I didn't think I was doing a very good job of hiding my expression, which I had a suspicion was a mix of yearning and bewilderment.

I startled when Magnus raised a hand. He waited, and when I didn't pull away again, he stroked my cheek. And then my brows. He brushed a thumb lightly over my lips.

I shivered and parted them.

Magnus sighed and dropped his hand.

"I wasn't disciplining the lads," he said evenly, moving off. He steadied me when I dashed after him and bumped into his side. "They were making noise because they were getting off."

I choked on my spit. "I know that," I said when I'd finished coughing. Magnus gently rubbed my back. "Obviously. That is exactly what people sound like when they're, you know. Having fun. I sound just like it."

"Do you, now?"

"Maybe a little, um." *Stop talking, Gary.* "My voice isn't all that deep? So maybe my cries of pleasure are higher? Than general?" *Stop it. Right now. No more talking.*

"Your...cries of pleasure?"

"Yes?" Had I phrased that wrong? Magnus sounded rather stunned. "Of...um. Ecstasy."

"Ecstasy."

He was just repeating my words now. "Yes," I said. "Ecstasy and completion and whatnot. Finding...finding the release. The climax. Of all the fucking."

Magnus stopped suddenly. He dropped his pack, picked me up off my feet and shoved me back against a broad tree trunk hard enough that I said, "Oof," and then, "What's wrong? *Is it a bear?*"

"No," Magnus said in a rough voice, and kissed me again.

This was even better than the first kiss.

I'd always been a quick learner and I was a natural at this, going on how Magnus was moaning—deep, rumbling noises that thrilled me down to my bones.

Magnus kissed me and kissed me, and I did it right back. Oh. Oh. I *loved* it.

I could do this all day long, I—

Magnus angled my jaw with a firm hand, tilted his head, and slipped his tongue into my mouth.

I bit him.

5

"Oh, fuckballs," Magnus said, jerking away.

"Sorry! I'm sorry! You startled me, I didn't know what was happening! I didn't mean to, it was a reflex, I—"

"It's okay," Magnus said. "Hush. Ssh. It's okay."

I pressed my forehead into Magnus' throat so I wouldn't have to look him in the eye as I slowly expired from embarrassment.

Magnus was still holding me against the tree and off the ground. He was probably getting tired with it.

I hitched my legs up and wrapped them around his waist. Moving around rubbed my back against the trunk and I flinched with a twinge of discomfort. While the thick greatcoat and the ridiculous clothes beneath provided some padding and protection, and the Wound of Betrayal was more of a Lightly Seeping Graze of Betrayal, it was still a tender spot.

Magnus muttered something soothing again and shuffled me about, rearranging his grip.

I pushed my shoulders into the tree, arching my back to keep the pressure off the sore spot.

Then he just held me.

"I'm sorry," I said again in a small voice.

"Don't apologise," Magnus said. "I shouldn't have pushed you. I know that you're inexp—"

I stiffened.

Magnus cleared his throat. "I know that you're cautious about letting people close."

"That's it entirely. Yes. I'm a cautious man. I like to think things through."

"Mm-hmm." Magnus shifted me again.

I sucked in a breath at the friction against my cock. My hips hitched.

Magnus hissed quietly. He leaned hard into me, pinning me.

I flailed, trapped between the tree and Magnus and very much liking the sensation, but I didn't get anymore of that intriguing friction.

I eventually stopped, my breathing short and loud.

Magnus was watching my face. His eyes were dark and hot on mine.

"Can I kiss you?" he said.

"Please do," I said, then pulled back so quickly I hit my head against the tree. "Ow. Um. Are you going to do the tongue thing again?"

"Was thinking about it."

"Oh."

"That okay? Or do you not want me to?"

"I don't know? I liked the beginning part. You have lovely lips. They feel so nice on mine."

"Thank you," Magnus said. It came out a bit strangled.

I'd hate for him to think I hadn't been enjoying myself. I gave his enormous bicep a bracing squeeze. "Very velvety."

Magnus didn't say anything this time. It was just a broken hum.

"So...the tongue thing. That's...that's normal, yes?"

"Lots of people like it."

"Right. You mean when you do it to them? Or...in general? As in, everyone's sticking their tongues in each other's mouths on a regular basis?"

"Well, I didn't invent it, Gary. It's a thing people do."

"It is. We do it," I agreed firmly. "Indeed we do. And obviously I already knew that. What happened was, I was startled because it escalated quickly. I'm ready for it this time."

"Are you?" Magnus sounded sceptical.

That might have had something to do with the way I was cringing back against the tree.

"Yes?"

Magnus didn't move.

"Yes!" I tried again.

It had startled me because I hadn't expected it. Mostly it had startled me because the confident stroke of Magnus' tongue over mine had made every nerve in my body snap to life, like a log on the library fire suddenly snapping out a shower of sparks and waking me from a daydream.

And these sparks were still racing around my body, lighting me up in places I was used to being asleep. It was all very extreme.

I wasn't used to extreme.

I didn't think about my body all that much, other than feeding it when I was hungry, and taking it for walks or doing my daily calisthenics when I was stiff. I tried not to think of it as if it was something separate from *Gary!* but the truth was, my body often felt more like a beloved pet than it felt like me.

When Magnus had kissed me, I suddenly found myself slammed inside my body, bewildered and unprepared for all the new sensations that were raging through it.

But I was prepared now.

Or at least I was willing to give it a try.

Kissing, and maybe even some of the other intriguing things I'd caught Magnus doing.

I'd spent more than a few wide-eyed hours listening to Magnus in the stables with the lads. Not on purpose. Never on purpose.

On one particularly memorable afternoon, I'd been in the hayloft, reading.

My brothers had recently brought a gaggle of friends to Silverleigh for a hunt, all of them as rowdy and unpleasant as my brothers were. Most of the party had passed out drunk at dinner the night before, and I'd decided to make myself scarce until the hangovers and worst of the tempers wore off.

As was my habit, I'd retreated to my favourite reading nook in the hayloft. I felt safe in the stables in a way I didn't anywhere in the house. I tried to tell myself it was because nobody would think to look for me there, but really, I always knew it was because the stables were Magnus' domain.

It was raining outside that day, and cosy and warm where I was. I'd been drowsing over a book when I was disturbed by the noises from a stall below.

I hunkered down in my nest of straw and blankets and diligently focused on my book, but the murmurs and the occasional slap of...something, I didn't know what, it sounded something like Cook tenderising chicken breasts by pounding them with a rolling pin...made it almost impossible. And it went on and on.

I hunkered deeper into my blankets to block out the sound, and ended up drifting into a short and uneasy sleep.

I'd had very strange dreams, filled with the phantom sensation of jolting and the sound of panting and low cries.

I'd woken up feeling cross and agitated, like I'd misplaced something but I wasn't sure what. My body was aching with tension.

I'd woken all the way up when the lad, Callin, had screamed like he'd seen a spider. He kept on wailing about it as I sat there, rigid and horrified, wondering if I should run down and offer my assistance, until he finally tailed off with a drawn-out groan.

There were a few wet noises—kissing, I'd thought grimly. I recognised that sound well enough—and a brisk slap, and Magnus had sent him on his way.

I'd peeped through the hatch and watched as Callin walked out of the stables, bowlegged beneath my wide eyes. He'd worn a daft smile on his handsome face, and his cheeks glowed poppy red.

Magnus, on the other hand, hadn't seemed all that ruffled by the whole event. He'd come into view, yawning. He stretched his big shoulders, fastened his breeches, and got back to work.

I had waited a full hour before I slunk down the ladder and sneaked back up to the house.

But despite all the noise and carrying on, Callin and all the other lads were always smiling like fools and happy when they left Magnus.

I was...curious.

"You may kiss me," I said, and quickly added when

Magnus gave me an unimpressed stare, "Please. And do feel free to put your tongue wherever."

Magnus closed his eyes briefly as if in pain. He cupped my chin, leaned in, and brushed his tender, lovely, velvety lips over mine.

He lifted away and returned with another soft press, a gentle glide, a delicate nudge. He did it all again, and again, and again.

I tried to keep my eyes open because Magnus really did look spectacular like this; he had a tiny frown between his thick dark brows, and his lashes lay in a heavy fringe on his flushed cheeks.

Despite not wanting to miss a single detail of the world-shaking experience, I found it harder and harder to concentrate. My eyes drifted shut.

Before long, I was chasing Magnus' lips every time he lifted away. I wound my fingers through the long damp hair at the nape of his heated neck, and squeezed my thighs to pull him closer.

Magnus began shifting restlessly against me. I moved in counterpoint. It was easy. So sweet and easy, it made me catch my breath, over and over until I was gasping.

I went where Magnus guided me with firm hands. He angled my head first to one side then to the other. The gentle scrape of his stubble over my skin was divine. He broke from my mouth for a moment to press hot kisses at the hinge of my jaw, across my throat.

I arched my neck, offering him all the access he wanted. He said something that vibrated over my skin. It was too deep and low to hear the words. I didn't even think it was a question, but I said yes anyway.

I breathed in, short and sharp, when Magnus softly sort of...lapped...at my lips until they parted for him. My body was responding in ways beyond my control or experience. It was terrifying. It was exhilarating. He played there until I was demanding more, pulling his hair with both hands.

Magnus shook against me with quiet laughter. So smoothly that I didn't even flinch, he slipped his tongue in and stroked softly over mine.

I made a mortifying honking noise through my nose.

Thankfully, Magnus didn't seem to notice.

He was busy cupping my whole face between his big hands, kissing me and now pushing his hips into me rhythmically.

I began to gasp and writhe in his hold.

The soft stroking of his mouth turned first demanding and then downright rude as his tongue drove in and he twisted it against mine.

In response, all of my muscles went pliant, loosening as if I'd slipped into a delightful, hot bath. I moaned and did my best to mimic Magnus' kiss.

His grip on me tightened. The demanding thrusts turned into a fierce claiming.

I was limp and shimmering with sensation at this point. If Magnus relaxed his hold even a fraction, I would simply slither to the forest floor. I welcomed him in—it wasn't unpleasant at all, what *had* I fussed about?—and I didn't even care when I realised that pleading whine came from my own throat.

Magnus rolled his hips into my hips at the same cadence as he rolled his tongue into my mouth.

I broke away to pant sharply into his neck. "Oh," I said. "Oh, Magnus, I think I'm—"

"Yes," Magnus said. "Yes."

My muscles seized, and everything drew down tight to a single pinpoint. Shuddering, I looked up and straight into

Magnus' wide-open eyes. They were fixed on mine, and although I tried, I couldn't tear my gaze away the whole time I reached completion.

Right in my breeches.

"Sorry," I said, when I'd stopped shaking and shivering in Magnus' steady arms. "Oh, *no*. I do apologise, I—"

"Shh." Magnus kissed me, his breath striking hard against my cheek. "Good, Gary. That was good."

I perked up. "It was?"

Magnus groaned, and stroked my hair back off my hot face.

"It was good, Gary," he said. "You did exactly what you were supposed to." Even though his words were approving, Magnus' expression was tense and harsh. He started to pull away.

I clung on. "Wait, what about you?"

Even I knew that this coupling business was supposed to go both ways.

"I'll take care of it," he said.

"Or I could?"

Magnus stilled. "You know what you're offering?"

"Of course I do."

I had no idea.

"Yeah?" Magnus slid an arm between the tree and my back and hupped me up.

"Absolutely."

"Tell me."

"I am..." I stalled for time, painfully aware of Magnus' thoughtful gaze on my face. "I am offering to, um, assist you in reaching completion."

"You want to make me come?"

My cheeks scorched.

Magnus reached out and ghosted the backs of his fingers

over my face, drawing a gentle line from my temple to the hinge of my jaw and along until he grasped my chin with warm fingers. He waited until I met his eyes before he said, "Is that what you want?"

"Yes?"

Magnus didn't seem all that convinced by my reedy reply.

Before he could pull away, I tried again. "Yes!" I barked.

I'd overcompensated. He bit his lip in amusement.

Crossly, I reached for Magnus' cock. Before I could lose my nerve, I squeezed my alarming handful and gave it a brisk, businesslike pull.

"Uhn." Magnus yanked me away with a pained grunt. He pressed his forehead into the tree trunk beside me, and panted.

I didn't think it was a good sort of panting.

6

After a minute of awkward silence—awkward on my part, at least, dangling there, feeling like a fool, while Magnus appeared to be gathering himself—he stepped back and eased me down.

Once on my feet, I cleared my throat and scuffed at the damp leaf litter mounded around the base of the tree.

It was clear as anything that I'd gone about the whole thing wrong.

Magnus didn't know I was utterly inexperienced and had no idea what I was doing.

He could think that I had hurt him on purpose.

Or that I was just not very good at it.

He could think any number of things, and none of them were good.

I shot him a look from under my lashes. At best, I expected irritation. At worst, I was braced for anger.

He was watching me with a tender expression.

My head came up and tilted questioningly.

"It's all right, Gary," Magnus said. With one hand at the

centre of my chest, he nudged me back against the tree. With the other, he undid his breeches.

I caught my breath. His lips, reddened and a little swollen from kissing, curved in a small smile.

His eyes glinting in the bright, clear moonlight, Magnus slid his hand into his breeches. I glanced down and couldn't look away when it started to move beneath the dark woollen fabric.

For a moment, I stared. Then I made another of those awful noises as I snatched hold of his hard hips. As quickly as I'd grabbed him, I let go. "Sorry."

"It's all right," Magnus said again. "You can touch me. I want you to."

"But I don't want to hurt you."

He grinned. "I won't let you." He sighed and flexed his body in a subtle, sensual roll.

A rush of arousal prickled over my skin, almost painfully.

Well. He couldn't say I didn't warn him.

Cautiously, I settled my fingertips on the back of his strong wrist where it was exposed by his shirt cuff, and savoured the rhythmic movement as he continued to work his cock. After a few strokes, I let my fingers drift down, out of sight, and over the back of his hand.

My stomach clenched hard at the shock of heat and the overwhelming intimacy of having my hand *inside* another man's breeches. "Oh."

Magnus laughed softly and shifted closer. He braced his free arm over my head and leaned into it, his attention warm and steady on my face. He was smiling at me with that bemused, tender curl to his lovely lips.

He paused the steady stroke, and let go of his cock to make room for me.

I wrapped my hand around it.

And that was about as far as my confidence could carry me.

I stood there holding his cock, breathing hard.

Until this moment, I'd never imagined that any softness could be found on Magnus' body, or that there was such a range of textures to be discovered. His lips were like velvet, his cock was like hot silk.

You couldn't tell by looking at him.

He looked nothing but solid, rough and hard.

My breathing, already mortifyingly loud, grew even louder when Magnus' hand covered mine and he resumed the slow, steady stroke.

I glanced up to check on the approval/you're doing it wrong situation.

He was waiting. "Like that," Magnus said in encouragement. His teeth dented his lower lip for a moment and his lids lowered. "Mhm. Like that. You're perfect." He continued to guide me with his firm, no-nonsense touch.

I grazed the full length of his scorching cock and he let me linger at the tip as I explored the incredible, blunt smoothness I found there with a tentative brush of my fingers.

Magnus hissed and his hips bucked, knocking into me and pinning me hard against the tree for a second before he pulled back.

I froze.

"It's good," Magnus said, his voice low and rumbling. "You're so good for me. Keep going. Gently."

"Okay."

Magnus released his hold on my hand bit by bit until I was confidently stroking him on my own. He seemed to like it when I paid extra attention at the tip, where he was leaking.

I made sure to stop and rub my thumb over the head every few strokes.

I'd done this to myself a few times, although I had the vague idea that I didn't do it even a fraction as much as other people did. I heard the stable lads and the gardeners gossiping. I heard my brothers and their friends boasting.

Some of them had talked about touching themselves two or three times a day, saying that if they didn't, their great big manly bollocks would explode.

That was hyperbole, of course.

Bollocks couldn't *actually* explode.

I knew that for a fact, since I was deeply alarmed when I'd first heard it. I'd continued to be deeply alarmed until I'd spent some time in the library and verified that they were talking absolute nonsense.

Being obliged to read up on the topic also verified that the whole business was, as I'd suspected, of minimal interest to me.

Once I'd assured myself that my lack of interest wasn't going to end in anything exploding because I wasn't dutifully jerking it three times a day, I paid it little to no attention.

I took care of my needs as and when they came up, which was infrequent, and that was that.

I hadn't ever been interested in myself that way.

I was, however, extremely interested in Magnus.

Compelled, I'd go so far as to say.

Right now, I'd slipped into something of an erotic daze, my unblinking eyes fixed on where my hand disappeared into his breeches, as I stared in the hope I might get to see something as well as feel it.

Magnus widened his stance, spreading his thighs and giving me more wiggle room.

All this thinking about bollocks prompted me to, when I'd next dragged my fist closer to the heat of Magnus' body, let go of his cock. Only for a moment. I didn't want to ruin the rhythm.

I wanted…

I wanted to…

I leaned in and rested my forehead against Magnus' chest.

I slid my hand lower and caught the weight of his balls in my palm. And they were weighty.

I closed my fingers around them to get a sense of the shape, and heard myself swallow wetly. Magnus made a faint noise above me. His restless hips hitched forward.

I quickly straightened and returned my attention to Magnus' cock. Perhaps if we did this again sometime—I was already hoping we would—Magnus would let me have more of a poke around. Perhaps in daylight.

Perhaps…perhaps even with his breeches off.

Best not to get ahead of myself, though. Mostly because the thought of Magnus standing this close, pressing against me with no breeches between us, made me lightheaded.

I'd already fainted once today.

When I glanced up again to check Magnus' expression, I saw that his eyes were locked on my face.

I blushed at the intensity of his attention.

Sighing, he bent to kiss my cheek before directing his gaze down to where I was holding his cock. I'd stopped stroking it to hold it for a moment, enjoying the heat and texture of satiny skin.

I felt his *heart*beat.

I rubbed my thumb absently along a thick, pulsing vein.

It was such a strange and intimate thing. Not the vein. Standing there in the dark and holding Magnus' cock.

I resumed stroking. This was another of those things that I was vaguely aware other people did differently.

Sometimes, it seemed as if everyone went around cheerfully and boisterously grabbing each others cocks and breasts.

When I turned fifteen and my spots cleared up, a few people had started trying to grab me. My brothers' friends. My father's largest tenant-farmer. My cousin. Twice removed, but still. My *cousin*.

I didn't bother mentioning it to my father. I'd learned early on that it was best not to remind him of my existence.

I did mention it to Gower, my favourite brother. Or, the least mean of them.

Gower had scoffed at me and said it was my own fault because I had lips like a whore and a girl's face.

I didn't see what my lips or my face had to do with people lunging for my cock *a propos* of nothing.

When I pressed him on it, Gower had gone a dull red and crossly told me to not let anyone get me alone in the first place, and I'd be fine.

It was a surprisingly elegant solution. No one ever got close enough again, and I didn't have to think about it from one year to the next.

Until Magnus.

Not only had I let Magnus get close, I was enjoying it. I wouldn't mind being closer, although I couldn't think how we'd manage it, since we were all but plastered together as it was.

All I knew was, I wanted more.

If I'd been doing it to myself, by now I'd have been frustrated that nothing had happened, and gone off to make a cup of tea and find a good book, but I was deliberately slowing down. Who knew when I'd get the chance to experience it again?

This was wonderful.

Magnus was wonderful.

I wanted to do it forever, even though my wrist was beginning to ache.

Magnus had both arms braced beside me now, caging me in. He breathed in heavy, rough-edged sighs as he rocked his hips.

Oh, that was nice.

His cock glided through my grip, and I got to feel the power of his thick thighs flexing against mine.

I boldly moved my free hand around to the small of his back. When Magnus didn't say anything, continuing to rock his hips, I touched his buttock.

Magnus rumbled something that sounded encouraging.

The blood was roaring in my ears at this point and I couldn't quite hear the words through the buzz of excitement, but I spread my fingers and squeezed.

Oh. Magnus' arse was almost as nice as Magnus' cock. A heavy, hard curve of muscle that I felt working under my palm.

Magnus was no longer gently rocking into my inquisitive grip. He was thrusting, his hips making powerful, demanding pushes. His deep sighs had become low growls.

Normally, a man growling at me would make me bolt, but this was Magnus. I was thrilled.

I fumbled at a particularly hard thrust, apologised, and regained my grip. Two hands might be better, I thought, considering the girth I was working with here.

I took hold with both.

"Fuck, yes," Magnus said on a moan. "Tighter—*not too tight.*"

I eased back. "Of course. How…is this all right?"

I cupped Magnus' magnificent hot cock in both hands, gasping at the feel of him sliding fast and rhythmically through my grip.

Magnus' thrusts grew lustier. His hips and thighs shoved and pushed into me, jostling me about in a new and arousing manner.

He kept leaning his upper body back so he could look down. His hungry gaze roamed over my face, down to where I held him, and back up.

I couldn't look away from his torso, especially when his shirt came untucked and I saw brief and shadowed flashes of his abdominal muscles tightening and releasing hypnotically.

There were noises. Rather wet noises at this point, considering how much Magnus was leaking, and barely audible under Magnus' loud, ragged pants.

And mine.

My breathing was the worst, and all I was doing was standing there doing my best to hang on to the slick cock working into my hands.

Every time Magnus pushed into me, his breath came out in a soft, rumbling *ah*!

My mouth was open as I gawked at what was happening.

Magnus was saying things like, *yes*, and *you're perfect*, and *like that, sweetheart. Yes, like that.*

I would have preened under the praise, only I couldn't look away or do anything but hold on as Magnus thrust faster and faster.

Without warning, he pulled sharply out of my hands, and made the wise decision to spend on the forest floor.

Unlike me.

I'd done it in my breeches, and I was having the first inklings of how unpleasant matters would soon become.

I watched, owl-eyed, as Magnus groaned and his whole body relaxed. He tucked himself away, cut me a wicked look, and scooped me up against his body. He kissed me, hard and fierce again, but disappointingly short.

"Thank you," he said. He pulled away to peck me on the lips, the nose, and the forehead. He let me go, and efficiently fastened his breeches.

"Ah. You're very welcome. Thank you also."

Magnus scratched his stubble and said ruefully, "I hadn't intended our first time to be up against a tree in the forest, just so you know. At night, no less. Come on. We'd best be going."

Our first time?

Intended?

That was all very intriguing, but I didn't ask him for more details. Now that my head was no longer filled with Magnus and my body was no longer throbbing with lust, I was back to worrying about bears.

Magnus hefted up his pack, slung it over his shoulder, and headed off. He glanced back and grinned at me expectantly.

I scurried after him, and kept close.

7
———

The moon rode higher and sharper overhead. Silver light spilled through the branches of the trees, bright and hard, cutting into the shadows.

"Are there wolves around here, too?" I asked. "As well as bears?"

"Yes, of course."

Fantastic. "Trolls?"

"Not this far south." I saw Magnus' small smile bloom in the darkness, a flash of white teeth. "I'll keep you safe, don't worry."

I trusted that Magnus would do his very best, but still. *Bears and wolves.* I sidled closer and bumped against him.

Even though we were in a random forest so very far from home, and even with the moon lighting our way, I couldn't see a path.

Magnus seemed to know exactly where we were headed.

His steps were purposeful. There was no dithering whatsoever. He simply forged on through the undergrowth and around the trees, stopping every now and then to hold back low branches or brambles for me.

"Where are we going?" I said.

"There's an inn I know a couple of hours walk from here."

A couple of *hours*?

I grimaced.

My clothes, my hair, and my skin were all wet and muddy. I wasn't even going to think about the state of matters inside my breeches.

Well, I tried not to think about it. Every step made me cringingly aware of it nonetheless.

I yearned for a bath. A hot bath, with bubbles.

And food.

The one good thing about my time as king was the bath.

The royal tub was three times the size of anything at home. It took the servants an hour to fill it, and I could request a top-up any time I wanted.

Sometimes, they gave me food with which to occupy myself during the royal soak. A cheese platter, with grapes, and wafer-thin slices of sweet, crisp apples.

"A couple of hours as in two?" I asked hopefully. I could manage two hours.

"A couple as in three. Or four." He caught my elbow as I tripped. "Or five."

"I'm sure if we went back to the road, we'd find an inn much sooner. And it wouldn't be such hard going."

"We would indeed. But any inn close to the main road is a posting inn, and there's a chance, however slim, that someone could recognise you. I'm not looking for unnecessary fights."

Apart from with bears and wolves, apparently. Those were not a problem for Magnus.

"It's not any old inn we're going to," he said. "We're not

wandering through the forest hoping to come across one, Gary."

I hadn't even thought about it. I was following him like a baby duck.

I sighed.

I'd follow him anywhere.

"It's been years since I passed through this way," Magnus said, "but I've stayed at The Red Cloak before. It's small, off the main routes and, for the right price, discreet."

"No one would even think I was me, would they?" I said, attempting to scale an enormous fallen tree that lay in our path. Magnus caught me around the waist when I stumbled, and righted me. I batted him away. "I can do it," I said.

He waited for me to scramble up, swing a leg over and slither down the other side, before he vaulted it with irritatingly casual ease.

Then again, I'd seen him run alongside a stallion in the paddock during a training session, and somehow fling himself onto its back without bouncing off and landing face first in the grass.

A tree trunk wasn't going to present much of a challenge to a man with those sort of skills.

I could barely mount a horse when it was standing still, waiting for me in the yard, *and* I had a boost.

There were many disadvantages to being shorter than average. At twenty-eight years of age, I'd rather optimistically thought I'd discovered them all.

Apparently not.

Giant fallen trees in the forest at night went on the list.

Then again, I was discovering all sorts of things today.

My 'friend' Drusan had been plotting my death before we'd even met.

I'd been a warmongering tyrant and the worst king in the history of the Kingdom of Estla to ever rule.

And I now knew how to bring a man off.

Exciting times.

"I mean, everyone thinks that I'm dead," I said to Magnus' broad back.

I had little hope that he'd give in and let me go back to the road, but it was worth a try.

"Wouldn't someone think I'm just a man with an unfortunate resemblance to the dead tyrant king?" I snorted and kicked the leaves. "Tyrant. Honestly." I threw up my hands. "How could I have been a tyrant? I never told anyone what to do, so where they came up with that I do not know. You want to see a tyrant? You should meet Nanny Haig. She was very strict. Very ready with the birch."

"Your nursemaid beat you?" Magnus ground out, his voice low.

"She made me hold out my hands and she tapped them with the birch rod, that's all. Nothing like Father."

Ahead of me, Magnus stopped dead and clenched his fists at his sides.

Startled by his sudden halt and alarming posture, I eased back.

"That makes me very angry, Gary," Magnus said. His voice was even lower. It was barely above a growl.

Nothing like the sexy growling he was doing earlier.

Not knowing quite know how to respond, I eased back a fraction more, and trod on a twig. It cracked loudly.

Magnus turned at the sound. He blinked. For some reason, he looked stricken. He held out a hand to me, his eyes dark and beseeching.

I'd only shifted away out of habit. I didn't think for a single moment that *Magnus* would lash out.

I quickly reached back and took his hand, tangling our fingers together.

Magnus reeled me in until I bumped into his body. He dropped a kiss on the top of my head.

He really was a sensitive man.

Fancy getting upset about me taking my punishment.

My brothers and I all had to.

In an attempt to distract him, I picked up the thread of our conversation.

It didn't hurt to make another bid for an inn sooner rather than later, either. My breeches were drying out, but matters were hardly improving.

"Even if people did give me a second look," I said, "there's no reason for them to think it was me-the-king. No doubt word has spread that everyone in the capital is toasting marshmallows at my funeral bonfire." I scowled. "I'm still offended that I didn't get a proper pyre."

"Takes time to build one," Magnus said with a shrug. "Drusan is a politician not an assassin. That amateur didn't even know to check he'd succeeded before he proclaimed himself the saviour of the kingdom. I'm sure he had big plans for your body. Probably some kind of display. He's a showman, after all.

"As it stands, your body vanished. His claim to have liberated Estla was invalidated within minutes. Without physical proof for the masses and more importantly for any other factions wanting to rule through you as a puppet, like he'd been doing, the only thing he could do was cover for his cockup by making it look like *he* made you disappear. Hence finding another body to burn, and doing it as quickly as possible."

I marvelled at Drusan's adaptability. He really was much better suited to being in charge than me.

He'd accomplished all of that since this morning, while all I'd done was steal a coat and boots, and end up being chased down a dark road by someone who, luckily, turned out to be Magnus.

But could have been a bear.

Of course, being a better ruler didn't mean Drusan was a good man.

He was still an absolute arsehole for stabbing me.

"Will it work?"

"He's giving the people what they want. A villain to blame, and someone to hate for the way he's been taxing them to fund his wars and schemes. A party." A vicious smile twisted Magnus' lips. "As for Drusan's long-term prospects? We'll see how it pans out. Personally, I don't give him more than a couple of months before it's his turn in the fire."

"Drusan of a Hundred Days," I mused. "I prefer that to Drusan the Liberator."

"Hmm. I doubt he'll reach your record."

"I did do rather well, didn't I?" I said. "I kept expecting to die every day, but I seemed to have the strangest flashes of luck."

Magnus grinned at me. "Luck, huh?"

"Yes. There was one time, a man died quite horribly when he drank from my goblet by mistake. He was standing right next to me, and we'd both just been served. Magnus, it was *poisoned*."

"How unfortunate for the poor man," Magnus said dryly.

"I know, particularly as I didn't even want a drink in the first place. He was the one insisting I try the claret as it was a very special vintage. Unique, he said. He assured me it would leave me gasping."

Magnus hummed.

"The servant must have got the goblets mixed up," I said.

"This is why you should be careful about who you hire, and make sure you pay folk the right sum for what they are being asked to do."

"I agree. Then there was another time. Some falling masonry barely missed me. I honestly didn't see much of what happened, because one of the footmen, not one I'd seen before and I suppose he lost his job because I didn't see him again after that, tripped over my robes and knocked me clear. I landed facedown, which I am very grateful for because I didn't have to see what happened to Lord Allen, who had invited me on the walk. I hear it was quite horrifying."

"Ah yes. Lord Allen. One of Drusan's closest cronies."

"That's the man. Always trying to take me on walks, even though I could tell he didn't like me very much. And then another time, I was reviewing the Royal Guard at their archery practice. It was one of them who interrupted this time, not a servant. He called out to me, I turned at the right moment, and the arrow missed me by a hair."

"I heard about that one, too."

I gazed off into the trees. "Poor Sir Lyman. He was another of Drusan's friends. He'd been standing right beside me, you know. It was his idea to review the guards. You wouldn't believe how far blood can squirt, Magnus. He took the arrow right to the neck."

I'd fainted, obviously.

No one had noticed, what with all the fuss and screaming, and the two guards who'd sprinted over and thrown themselves on top of me. I'd regained consciousness before they climbed off and hustled me back to the Palace.

"Whoever Drusan was hiring," I said, "he really should

have chosen a better caliber of assassin. It was almost as if someone was watching over me."

"Almost, huh?" Magnus lifted my hand to his lips and pressed a smiling kiss to the back of it.

My knees weakened and I turned my wrist in his grip to rest my palm against his cheek and gaze into his sparkling, knowing eyes.

I was so busy being thrilled at his tender gesture that it took a moment to dawn on me what all that sparkling meant.

With a sudden lurch of my stomach, I remembered what he'd said on the road earlier.

I was bribing half the fucking city to keep me informed of your movements, Drusan's movements, Palace gossip. The works. Servants, guards, street rats, society ladies, lords, clerks, ministers. I made sure that if anyone so much as whispered your name, I'd hear about it.

"Oh my gods," I said blankly. "It was you? You were the one foiling all the plots?"

"Of course it was me."

"But...I don't...I don't understand why..."

"Yes, you do."

"I don't!"

"Then you're saying that you can imagine a world where I watched you drive away, and didn't come after you? A world where the news of what was going on in the capital finally reached Silverleigh, and I thought of you there, knowing that you would die alone and afraid, and I carried on with my daily business? You can imagine a world where I didn't even care. Where—"

I slapped my hand over his mouth, startling him. That sounded *awful*. "No."

He pulled my hand away and placed it on his chest instead.

His heart beat steadily beneath my palm. Mine was racing. My skin everywhere felt stretched tight, my pulse fluttering and knocking against it from the inside.

Magnus' gaze softened. "You'll understand when you're ready," he said. He chucked my chin, breaking the heavy tension, and moved off. "Come on. I don't know about you, but I'm more than ready for bed."

"Oh, a bed." I sighed gustily. "I feel like I've been walking in these horrible boots since the beginning of time."

"That's quite a while."

"It is. And I'd like to stop before all the blisters pop."

"I can carry you."

He had come after me, spent three months foiling attempts on my life, and was now on the run with me.

I refused to make the man literally carry me.

Even though the thought of curling up in his arms was very tempting.

"Or," I said, "we stop at the closest inn rather than going cross-country to this other one. I really don't think anyone will recognise me. I saw the posters they had of me in Jarra. The pictures were all so refined and beautiful and cruel." I gestured at myself. "And I'm so very ordinary."

Magnus' step hitched.

Hah. Nice to see that I wasn't the only one stumbling around in the dark.

"Your appearance is quite distinctive, Gary," he said.

He could only be talking about one thing.

"Are you saying that because I'm short?" I demanded. "Because I'll have you know that I've researched extensively, Magnus, and while I am indeed below average height, it's not by *that* much. Besides, average is a shocking measure of incidence. I infinitely prefer a median."

Magnus shook his head with a rumble of laughter. "It's the whole package," he said fondly, running a hand up the back of my neck and ruffling my damp curls. "You're a recognisable man."

That was absolute nonsense, but I didn't see any use in arguing the point. Not when I had another point I was much more interested in arguing.

"I think that you're being overly cautious. I'm not sure I can stand another five hours of this."

I pulled at my breeches in discomfort, trying to ease the fabric away from my skin. It kept dragging over my parts and was most unpleasant.

Things were becoming tacky and beginning to stick.

"That'll teach you to come in your underwear," was Magnus' unsympathetic remark.

I gaped at him. "It was *your* doing!" I said. "You should have warned me. How was I to know?"

"How indeed?" Magnus murmured with another of those fond smiles.

Realising that I was revealing my ignorance, I backtracked. "Obviously, I *know*. Because it happens all the time."

"All the time, huh?"

"Oh, yes," I said breezily. "Five times a week?" I checked Magnus' expression. I saw a tell-tale (lovely) dimple of amusement, but no hint of surprise on his face.

I assumed that I'd estimated well.

"Yes, five times a week. It's one of those things, I suppose, that we must put up with, being men. Uncomfortableness in one's drawers."

Magnus caught his bottom lip between his teeth and chewed it briefly. "Mm-hmm." He nodded.

"But it would be nice not to feel so, uh. Out of sorts. Down there. And sooner rather than later?"

"No," Magnus said, and I knew that tone of voice. He'd never used it on me before, but I'd heard him use it on everyone else, from the stable lads to the stallions. There was no arguing with him. "You'll be recognised. And we're going to have to do something about that if we're to get you all the way over the border."

"We're leaving Estla?"

"Yes," Magnus said firmly, as if he'd expected me to disagree with him.

I was fine with it.

I didn't see any point in staying in a kingdom that had risen up, and in one voice said, *He's dead. Huzzah.*

On that note... "If you truly think that there's a chance people will recognise me, do you think we should do something to disguise my appearance? Is an out-of-the-way inn enough caution?"

The thought of being captured and then being either dragged back to the Palace in shackles for a ceremonial killing, or despatched on the quiet and left for wild animals to dispose of, was less than appealing.

The thought of being taken away from Magnus? Strangely worse.

Fingering my curls, I said, "We should cut my hair." My shoulders slumped. "Best to shave my head, actually."

"Let's not go too far," Magnus said.

"We could dye it, then? Brown like yours sounds nice." Magnus had a mane of rich chestnut a few shades darker than his eyes, with intriguing streaks in it, of silver and gold.

A half-smile curled his lips. "It does?"

"Yes. Where will we find the dye, though? Hmm. Good strong coffee will muddy it up nicely. Oh!" I turned to walk backward in front of Magnus a few steps. He reached out and cupped my elbows. I hung onto his forearms. "Don't ever tell, but Mrs Robards makes a tincture of crushed walnut shells to colour her greys. We could do that." I glanced around at the trees. It was a mixed forest, mostly deciduous, heavy on the birch and the oak. No walnut in sight. "They'll probably have plenty of nuts at the inn."

"I'm sure they'll have all the nuts we could want. Luckily, we can stick to eating them, and use the hat I bought you."

"Ah. Yes, a hat. That's easier than shaving it or dyeing it, I suppose. Though I think I could look quite sophisticated as a brunet."

I released Magnus' forearms and turned to walk alongside him, facing the right way.

I kept hold of one of his hands.

After a few steps, I glanced up. He didn't look at me but he was smiling, and he squeezed my fingers.

"You bought me a hat?" I said, oddly touched.

"Among other things."

"Where is it?"

He silently shrugged the shoulder he'd slung the pack over.

"You've got things in there for me, too?"

He huffed. "Gary, I've had a bag packed for the two of us and standing by the door of my lodgings from the second I arrived in the city, ready to leave at a moment's notice."

"That's very thoughtful of you. Very organised."

Very not like me.

I'd just seized that moment and run.

We walked on in silence.

My steps began first to drag, and then to falter.

Magnus offered to carry me again, and while I was even more tempted, I did have some pride left.

An endless trudge later, Magnus allowed us finally to come out of the forest, through the thinning trees and onto a narrow road that was more pothole than path. I twisted my ankle three times before he lost his patience and hauled me up and over his shoulder.

He'd tried to carry me like a damsel at first, but I kicked and complained until he tossed me up and over like a bag of grain.

His heavy shoulder dug into my midriff and I had to fight for space with the pack on his other shoulder. I kept hitting my face on it. I wished I'd kept my mouth shut and endured being cradled like a precious lady.

One more thing to learn today.

After only another twenty minutes on the road, Magnus gave a satisfied grunt, and turned so I was facing forward long enough to catch the welcome gleam of warm yellow light in the distance.

Magnus clapped a hearty hand on my backside and lengthened his stride. "Be there before you know it," he said.

It started to rain again.

I didn't bother to ask if we could stop for the hat.

I sighed, and consoled myself with watching the bunch and flex of Magnus' arse as we trudged on.

8

The Red Cloak inn was small and set back from the road. It was old and shabby, with a lopsided roof of slate that shimmered like black water under the rain, and tiny mullioned windows that beckoned with a warm yellow glow. By the time we arrived it was past ten, and the taproom was mostly empty when Magnus squelched in with muddy boots.

He slid me off his shoulder and propped me in the shadowed corner opposite the long, low hearth. Exhausted, I leaned gratefully against the lumpy plaster wall.

My coat was streaming with rain but I didn't think it would matter all that much—the plaster was dingy, pocked with age, and had a faint bluish bloom of mould creeping up from the floor. Another damp patch wasn't going to ruin things.

I could barely stand up on my trembling legs anyway. So it was moot.

I watched as Magnus crossed the room with that no-nonsense, confident stride of his.

Now *there* was a man with the bearing of a king.

Not a jewelled king of courts and ballrooms like Drusan, nor the haughty, arrogant kind of king that they'd painted me as. He simply had a bone-deep certainty and authority, the kind that had people doing his bidding without question.

I never did get the hang of it.

Even when I was just a lord.

Magnus had a short conversation with the barkeep, handed over a purse so heavy that I heard it clink even from across the room, and then he was back and guiding me up the stairs with a warm hand at the base of my neck.

I cast a wistful glance over my shoulder.

Three of the tables were occupied. I was more interested in the food that occupied it than the people.

"I'm having soup and bread sent up," Magnus said in amusement. "I don't want you sitting down there where people can get a good look at you. We haven't shaved your head yet."

"I look like a drowned rat. A muddy, wretched, drowned rat. And I thought we weren't shaving my head?"

Magnus pushed me ahead of him, and all but ran me up the stairs.

I was breathless by the time we reached the darkness at the top, although that was due less to the speed and more to his proximity and the dawning realisation that we were about to be alone, and with no risk of bears to distract me.

At the top of the stairs Magnus moved past me, catching my hand and drawing me after him down the unlit, narrow passage towards a faint glow. "This way."

A small boy popped out of a door at the far end. "Fire's lit for you, sir," he informed Magnus as he scurried past us. "And the lamps. I'll be back up with your grub."

Magnus nodded at him, but the boy was already gone

and clattering down the stairs.

"Here we are," Magnus said. He stopped at the open door and gestured me to precede him.

"Thank you," I said.

The room was surprisingly large. It had bare wooden boards, a rug by the hearth, a lamp on a small table by the door and another lamp casting a cosy glow over the bed.

The very small bed.

It was going to be a tight fit with two of us in there.

I stared at it, hesitating, until Magnus scooted me forward with gentle pressure at the small of my back.

Once over the threshold, I caught sight of the fire in the hearth and any hesitation vanished. I kicked off my boots and ran for it, hands outstretched.

I changed course the moment I spotted the wooden bathtub crammed into a deeply recessed alcove.

A *bath*. Praise the gods!

I skidded to a halt beside it in my soaked stockings. It was empty.

"I'm having water sent up with the food," Magnus said.

"Will it...?" I trailed off into silence and fidgeted. I knew I was being demanding, but I felt so bad. *So* tired and disgusting, and still emotionally smarting from that whole stabbing incident.

A little splash of hot, clean water would go a long way to restoring my cheerful spirits.

"Will it what?" Magnus prompted.

I shrugged. "Nothing. It doesn't matter."

I already felt guilty enough that Magnus had carried me along the road for the last twenty minutes. I wasn't going to demand the water be heated.

I would dunk myself in cold water if cold water was all that arrived.

I was so desperate to be clean that I'd briskly rub myself down with ice, if ice was all that was on offer.

And I'd be brave about it.

Of course, I'd prefer hot water. Warm. Tepid, even. I didn't *want* ice.

I wrapped my arms around my chest and moved over to the fire. Getting warm now would make the chilly ablutions headed my way feel even worse, but I had been cold for long enough.

"It will be hot water, if that's what you're fretting about," Magnus said directly behind me.

I startled.

"Let's get your wet things off," he said.

I obediently wriggled out of the greatcoat. Magnus helped, easing it off my shoulders and down. If I hadn't been desperately relieved to get out of the horrible thing, I'd have been self-conscious at having him looming behind me.

The coat fell from his hand to the floor by my feet with a wet whump.

Magnus' breath came out in a shattered sigh.

I held still, my chest tight, and stared at the ruby and amber flames dancing over the huge log in the hearth.

I knew what Magnus was looking at: the long rent in the back of my frock coat where Drusan's knife had gone in, and torn downward.

"Gary," Magnus said, his voice low and angry. "You said you pretended to be dead. You didn't say that they *stabbed* you first!"

"Um." I started to turn. "Did I not...?"

"No, you did not." Magnus gripped my hip to keep me in place. He stepped closer, looping an arm around my waist, and setting his other hand at the base of my neck, urging me to bend and expose my back. "Why didn't you say anything?" His hand slid down my spine to between my shoulders, and I felt the light pressure of fingers trace the length of the rent.

I twisted away out of reflex with a hiss.

His arm tightened. "Shh," he said. "I'm not going to hurt you."

"Well, I know that," I said. "You surprised me. It tickles."

"I need to look at it, all right? Will you let me look?"

"Of course."

I jerked when he slipped his fingers through the ragged tear. He hummed quietly and I settled, standing there clutching the strong forearm around my waist with both hands.

"It's shallow," he said, tilting me toward the fire for a better look. "Gods. They shouldn't have been able to get so close." My hair was drying, and his heavy breath shifted it. His arm around me tightened. "No one should have been able to get this close. I didn't hear a word of an impending attempt. No one was hired. I don't understand how—"

"You wouldn't have heard anything," I said. "Drusan did it himself."

Magnus was utterly silent behind me.

"Drusan did it himself?" He bit the words out. "He was the one to stab you?"

"Yes."

There was another long, furious silence.

"He's a vicious politician and a ruthless First Minister," Magnus said eventually. "He's been playing this long game for years, going through royals like Death itself and somehow managing keeping his hands clean. But he's a shite assassin."

I huffed.

"Fuck. The man must have been at the end of his damn

rope and desperate to end it. I heard them calling him the Liberator this morning in Jarra when I was chasing after you, but I never thought for a second he'd have the balls to step onto the stage and show himself." Magnus' voice lowered. "They're going to eat him alive."

"Who?"

"Everyone," he said. "Anyone who, like Drusan, thinks that they'd do a better job of ruling. Who thinks that wanting it means they deserve it. Power's up for grabs now. Drusan doesn't realise it yet, but that fool just rang the dinner gong. They'll all come running."

I shivered.

"Gods, you should have told me about this earlier. Does your wound hurt? Is it sore? It had better not be infected." He sucked in a breath. "I was shoving you against that tree!"

"It's a scratch," I said. "A graze. Nothing to worry about. These ridiculous clothes took the brunt of it, I promise, and I enjoyed the tree very much."

"Nothing to worry about?" he echoed. "*Gary.*"

I patted his arm soothingly. "It's fine."

"I can't understand how he'd get this close, and not drive it home."

"I may have inadvertently made him think that I was wounded more, uh, fatally than I actually was?"

Magnus was silent behind me.

I heaved a sigh. "I fainted."

"You...?"

"It's stupid, I know, but I fainted. I faint at the sight of blood. There. Now you may make fun of me."

"I'd rather make fun of Drusan for not checking you were dead. He really is a fucking shite assassin." He cleared his throat. "Right. I'm going to rip it and get a closer look."

"Go ahead," I said when he didn't do anything.

"Ready?"

I laughed. "Yes! I hate these clothes, I don't even—"

I flinched and jerked forward reflexively at the awful sound of cloth ripping and the tug of it that pulled me backward. I closed my eyes tightly, trying not to see Drusan's smiling face as I looked up from my bloody hand.

I gripped Magnus' forearm, my nails biting into the cold, damp wool of his coat.

"You're right," he said after a heavy moment. He laughed in disbelief. "It's a scratch." He touched my skin softly. "A spot of soap and water will see you right."

"I had worse that time Embray threw me into the rose bushes," I said.

My mother's roses were old and fierce, with thorns the size of the tip of my thumb. Embray had picked me off my feet and tossed me right in the middle.

I don't remember what had prompted it, but a fair bet was I'd been asking him too many questions.

It had taken me a painstaking hour to unhook the thorns from my tattered clothes and skin and fight my way out of the bushes.

It had taken Mrs Robards and her best tweezers another two hours to pick out all of the smaller thorns that had broken off and stuck in my skin, as I writhed and complained in the stillroom.

When she got my shirt off, I'd been covered all over with long, oozing cuts.

That was how we learned I fainted at my own blood. Repeatedly.

Magnus' arm beneath my clutching fingers tensed and released.

"You should have been safe until I got you out," he said. "Thank the gods you got yourself out. I can't...I can't even think what would have happened if..." He trailed off into silence.

"Magnus?" I asked when it became clear he wasn't going to say anymore.

His hand was warm and steady, pressed flat to my back. His fingers were spread wide. It felt like he was framing the ridiculous scratch.

"Magnus?" I said again. "What happens now? Are we going home?"

Before he could answer my forlorn question, someone thumped on the door.

Magnus tugged me into his hard body in a quick little squeeze of reassurance, then strode across the room with purposeful steps.

A harried-looking maid stood outside with a steaming bucket held in each capable hand.

As soon as Magnus had opened the door for her, she booted it wider and muscled past him, heading straight for the wooden bathtub.

I attempted to contain my excitement.

The maid emptied the buckets one after the other into the tub, grabbed them, and headed back out.

Halfway across the room, she glanced at me, hovering by the hearth, and did a comical double-take.

My panicked gaze flew to Magnus. Shit. Had she recognised me?

The maid said, "Hello, there."

"Hello," I replied cautiously.

She didn't curtsey or look overwhelmed at being in the presence of royalty. She did give me a thorough looking-over, though.

"Right, then," she said, and tossed her thick braid over her shoulder before slowly dragging her gaze up off my abdomen where it had seemed to get stuck for some reason. Probably because my waistcoat hung open and showed the damp shirt plastered to my skin. "I'll be back with two more loads of hot water, but it cools quickly. If you want the bath nice and hot-like, you'd best go ahead and strip, and jump on in. I won't peek. Swear."

She gave me another lingering assessment then marched out.

"Do I look that wretched?" I asked Magnus.

He tipped his head from side to side in consideration, eyes gleaming. He didn't say anything.

I looked awful. I knew it.

I dutifully began to strip out of my clothes as the maid had suggested. I fought my way out of the frock coat and waistcoat, and peeled off my stockings, hopping from one foot to the other. I got to work on my shirt, but Magnus came over and stopped me before I had undone more than the top button.

The maid rushed in eagerly with the water. She slowed her steps when she saw that I hadn't moved from the fire. She emptied the buckets, staring at me as the water glugged noisily in. "One more load," she said. She bent down to test the water, and tutted. "It's getting cool already. Get your kecks off, lad."

Lad? I thought indignantly. She looked about eighteen! Ten years my junior, at least!

I also thought she was worrying overmuch about the water temperature. Great billows of steam wreathed up from the deep wooden tub. "I'll wait, thank you," I said primly.

It had sunk in that Magnus was about to see me naked. Or at the very least hear me being naked as I bathed.

I didn't need the maid seeing it, too.

She disappeared and soon trudged back with the last two buckets. She emptied them, and took a small ceramic dish from her pocket and set it on the floor beside the tub. "Some of the good soap for you," she said. "Smells real pretty."

She eyed me and left, colliding in the doorway with the boy from earlier, who was all but invisible behind the tray piled with bowls of soup and a heap of sliced bread and cheese.

Magnus closed and latched the door firmly behind them and came back to me, carrying the tray.

"Food first?" he asked. "Or bath?"

"I'm not that hungry anymore," I said. Now that food was in reach and not a vague hope for the future, the sharp edge of it had subsided. "Bath, definitely," I said, and made a move for the tub.

Magnus caught my hip and held me in place. Perhaps I should have minded it, being casually manhandled. I didn't. I glanced up at him in question.

He didn't say anything. He began to unbutton my shirt.

"Oh. Thank you." I squinted down and watched Magnus' long, capable fingers steadily working the buttons free, one by one. They were tiny, fiddly little things. Probably why this was taking such a long time.

I'd been assisted to dress and undress before. First by Nanny Haig, who was brisk and impatient. She'd stopped helping when I reached the age of five, telling me it was long past time to grow up, and that even spoilt little brat lordlings should be able to work out how to use buttons, and until they did, they weren't allowed out of the nursery.

The Palace servants had attempted it once. There, at least, I'd put my foot down.

Being undressed by Magnus wasn't remotely the same.

Remotely.

My chest squeezed and my heart started to pound, slow and sweet. I stood there compliantly, arms hanging uselessly at my sides, fingers flexing now and then. I didn't quite know what to do with my hands.

The warmth of the fire began to sink in and my head grew cloudy.

Magnus finished unbuttoning the shirt, and he stroked the panels aside. I sucked in a sharp breath at the brush of gentle fingertips sweeping over the sensitive skin of my abdomen.

"What is it?" I said when he curled his hands around my waist only to tip me back an inch and stare down. "What's wrong?"

"Wherever did you get these, my beautiful boy?" Magnus said wonderingly, and traced a forefinger across my lower abdominal muscles, then down the lines at my hips.

Beautiful boy? My heart skipped and I shifted awkwardly.

Magnus continued to hold me.

Should I take offence at being called boy? It felt very different from the maid calling me lad, and that feeling didn't have anything to do with Magnus being older. "Do you mean my muscles?"

Magnus flicked his gaze up for a second before he went back to staring at my stomach. He gave a single nod.

My cheeks heated with self-consciousness. "Um. I do calisthenics. Every day. Twice a day."

Magnus continued to stare. And stroke. My stomach jumped beneath his touch, but I didn't ask him to stop.

"For how long?" Magnus said.

"Ah, a couple of years."

He flashed me a quick, rueful smile. "I meant how long per day do you do these calisthenics?"

I laughed. "Not that long. Maybe an hour in the morning and an hour at night? Oh, I also do exercises to increase my flexibility."

I heard Magnus swallow. "Flexibility?" His voice was faint.

"Yes. I came across a book in the library once, with a section on all sorts of exercises designed especially for young men."

It seemed to be a compendium or manual of health and social graces, and was the same book I'd been obliged to investigate when I was worrying about exploding bollocks.

There was actually a number of similar books on that shelf, all hidden away at the very top of the bookcase. I was lucky to have found them.

I didn't know why they were so out of reach, since they were all specifically for young men who wanted to learn how to be pleasing and graceful. You'd think my father, with four sons he disliked and constantly berated for being disappointments and disgraces, would have put those books directly in our paths, rather than having them secreted away up there.

"I can do things like bend over and put my hands flat on the floor, or hold my ankles. That's good for the spine. And if I have time to warm up, I can get my legs very far apart in a straddle. It's a wonderful stretch for the inner thighs. Or I can get them tucked in right up by my ears. I don't do all of the exercises. Some seemed unnecessary. And peculiar, to be honest. I don't see why I need to strengthen things internally. I feel like everything's doing a good job of staying where it should without extra tight, um." *Sphincters*, I didn't say. It had all got very anatomical. I'd ignored all the puzzling illustrations, and flipped past quickly. "I like to stay healthy."

"You look, ah..." Magnus trailed off, made a considering noise at the back of his throat, and finally said, "Very healthy."

"Thank you." My fingers had curled around Magnus' wrists where he was still holding me. I wanted, suddenly and ridiculously, for him to call me *beautiful boy* again. He didn't.

He continued to hold me, circling his thumbs absently for a moment longer. Then he blew out an amused breath, shook his head, and without warning, whipped my breeches down my thighs.

I reflexively hunched over, covering myself.

Magnus went to his knees and dragged my breeches all the way down. He tapped my bare thigh briskly, like I was a horse. "Lift."

I braced myself on Magnus' burly shoulder and stepped out of the breeches one leg at a time.

He stood slowly, up and up. He was standing close, and I had to tip my head back to grin up at him when his knees cracked loudly.

"I could show you some exercises that are excellent for lubricating your joints," I said, daring to tease.

Magnus' level expression didn't change.

My smile grew.

His lips twitched. "Brat," he said, and ruffled my hair. He turned me around and slapped me on the bare arse. "Get into the tub. I'm after you and I don't want the water cold."

Relieved to have at least the semblance of privacy, I scampered over to the tub, leaped in, and let out a long, looooong moan of delight as I sank down to my chin.

When I was done with moaning my appreciation, I glanced up to find Magnus sitting at the end of the bed a few feet away, staring at me.

9

I sank down to my nostrils.

Magnus continued to stare.

I ducked below the water bashfully. I loved baths, and I wouldn't apologise for it.

I could feel foolish about it, though.

When I resurfaced, I scraped my wet hair off my face and blinked the water from my eyes. I reached an arm over the edge of the bath and grabbed the soap.

It *did* smell pretty. Like lavender, but cut with something a little darker that stopped it from being too overpoweringly flowery.

I turned the small bar briskly over and over between my palms until I had a double handful of bubbles, and started off with soaping my chest.

I shot another quick look over at Magnus. His face was red.

He hadn't taken his greatcoat off yet. It was getting toasty in the room, what with the crackling fire in the hearth and the steam rising from the tub and wreathing around me.

"I won't be long," I said. "If you want to start getting undressed, that is. Or you can wait, and I'll undress you."

It was kind of Magnus to have helped me. I'd like to return the favour.

As soon as I finished speaking, Magnus lunged to his feet, wrenched his coat off and hurled it away. He strode across the room.

My mouth opened as I watched the coat go. Not in the mood to wait, then.

I turned back to Magnus in time to have my chin caught in a hard hand, and lifted. Magnus crashed to his knees by the tub—he really shouldn't do that, the way they were cracking a moment ago—made an oddly desperate sound, and then he was kissing me.

He did the thing with his tongue, right away. I was ready for it this time, and I responded with enthusiasm.

Magnus cradled my face between hard palms and licked deep, deep into my mouth. Glorious though it was, my neck was at an uncomfortable angle. I made a quiet whimper of protest.

Magnus immediately stopped kissing me—*not* what I'd wanted at all—and snatched his hands away.

Since I'd twisted at the waist and balanced awkwardly on one hip to push up into the kiss, being released so suddenly had the unfortunate result of sending me sliding beneath the water.

"Oh, dear," I said when I came back up.

Magnus was drenched.

I peered over the edge of the tub. It seemed he'd caught the worst of it. Hopefully the water wasn't dripping through the floorboards and into the room below.

We'd hear about it soon enough if it was.

I plucked Magnus' sodden shirt away from his wet skin

and tugged gently. "You should probably take that off," I said.

Magnus was still kneeling beside the tub. He smiled slowly. "Yeah?"

I nodded.

His dark eyes steady on my face, Magnus began to unbutton his shirt.

He wasn't half as tender about it as he'd been with me.

In fact, it was less an unbuttoning and more an impatient ripping.

One button pinged off to roll over the bare floorboards and out of sight under the bed. Another two dropped into the tub with a tiny splash. He got it undone and yanked out of his waistband with impressive speed.

What lay beneath was infinitely more impressive. I felt my eyes widen.

Magnus' broad chest was heaving. He had wide shoulders above thick slabs of muscle. His muscles weren't as defined as mine, but then he did real work, not calisthenics designed to stop me developing the stooped posture of a man who spent too much time curled up with his books and journals.

Rather more interestingly, where I was smooth, Magnus had hair on his chest. I ran my fingers over my own chest thoughtfully, wondering what that would feel like to rub against.

Magnus' hands went to his breeches as he rose up to a high kneeling position. He stopped.

My attention had been locked on his breeches, scant inches from my rapt face. I was more than ready to see the magnificent cock I'd touched earlier. At Magnus' sudden stop, I looked up.

I couldn't read his expression at all.

I didn't fool myself I got it right half the time when I tried, but this was new territory for me. I couldn't even begin to make a guess.

I'd been lounging full-length in the tub like a wanton, spread out before him. Sitting up, I drew my knees to my chest and wrapped my arms around them. Tucked comfortingly tight, I set my chin on my knees and contemplated Magnus.

Magnus contemplated me back.

A strange, waiting kind of silence fell between us. I would have loved to break it, but for the life of me, I couldn't scrounge up a thing to say.

Magnus' voice was rougher and lower than usual when he finally did speak. "Gary," he said.

A flurry of goosebumps rushed over my damp skin.

He dipped a hand into the bath and trailed it a few inches here, a few inches there in the hot water, close to but not quite touching me. Slipping it deeper under the surface, he caught my ankle and gave it a light squeeze. "You know what I want from you?" he said. "You know what I'm going to take?"

I decided to try out being a brat again. I'd enjoyed it earlier. I thought about snipping back something like a cottage of his own on the estate and double the salary, but thought better of it at the dark, heavy look in Magnus' eyes.

Not the right moment.

He stroked his thumb over my ankle bone. I swallowed hard. "Um. You want to fuck me like you fuck the stable lads?"

Magnus shook his head slowly. "No."

Well.

That was both unexpected and potentially the most embarrassing moment of my life.

It was saying a lot. I'd had more than a few.

"Right, then." I uncurled and grabbed the soap, lathering it with a brisk nod. "In that case, no. I have no idea what you want. Except from wanting me to get on with it and get out of the tub, of course. If you'll give me a minute, I'll hurry up and—"

I stopped when Magnus slid a hand around the back of my neck and hauled me over to the side. The tub was rough wood and I was pretty sure I just got a splinter in my arse.

I didn't mention it.

"Do you know how long it's been since I fucked one of the lads?" Magnus said.

"You said that you were in Jarra for the full hundred days of my reign of terror, so...a hundred and one?"

Magnus gave me one of his flat stares.

I tried a smile. I'd noticed that, curiously enough, it tended to work.

Magnus blinked and his dimple popped.

It was really a deep crease in his stubbled cheek, stubble which I was itching to feel abrade my palms sooner rather than later, but I liked to call it a dimple. It made him seem more approachable.

Had he seemed any less approachable, I'd have been too intimidated to let him anywhere near me.

Especially not two scant inches away.

While I was wet and naked before him.

Magnus snorted and said, "Do you remember falling off Hazlette?"

"Ah. Could you narrow that down for me? At all? I've done it rather a lot."

Magnus grinned. I couldn't resist. I reached out and put my finger in his dimple.

He stilled beneath my touch, then reached up and

caught my hand. He pressed a hard kiss into my palm, wove our fingers together, and held our clasped hands to his chest.

His heart beat, fast but steady.

"The time you dislocated your shoulder," he said.

"Yes. I remember it."

Magnus raised his eyebrows. He seemed to be waiting for more.

I obliged. "I wasn't paying attention, which I always should be doing *at all times, my lord, head on a swivel—*" he'd told me often enough, "—and when Hazlette shied and ran because of the cat, I fell off onto the cobbles and my shoulder popped out."

"She didn't run." Magnus stroked my hair off my face and tucked it behind my ears. It was probably drying funny. He left his hands resting either side of my neck. "She walked briskly. You fell like a lump."

"It's one of the reasons why I started to do calisthenics. It seemed like a good idea. Strengthen the joints, learn how to fall."

I'd heard the crack of bone, too. As if dislocating my shoulder wasn't bad enough, I'd also managed to land on my wrist. It wasn't my first broken bone, but it never got easier. It sounded horrible, like a twig snapping underfoot.

All in all, it hadn't been a good day.

Magnus had been standing in the shadows of the stables, watching me ride in, as he always did. He'd been working there for three years by then. I thought it was a blow to his pride that I continued to be such a terrible rider despite all the instruction he, and all the stable lads gave me.

He was always there whenever I mounted to rearrange my shocking position—*heels* down, *my lord*—and there again when I returned, to quiz me and the unfortunate stable lad who'd been conscripted to accompany me on how the ride had been.

I was used to his watchful presence, but I'd never grown accustomed to it.

One of the cats came streaking out of the stable block and darted straight under Hazlette's enormous hooves. She sidestepped, snorting in surprise. She went one way, and I with my weak seat and abysmal grip on her barrel-like sides went the other.

Magnus had crossed the stable yard in less than a second, reaching me even before the lad riding alongside had leaped down.

"You looked at me like you wanted to throttle me," I said.

"No, sweetheart. I wanted to throttle myself for letting you get hurt. I looked at you like I wanted to never let you be hurt again."

"Oh. Hmm." I dropped my gaze from the intensity on Magnus' face.

Sweetheart. *Oh.*

"Well, I thought you were cross," I said.

"Yes. You apologised. A lot."

"Of course I did. You had to shove my shoulder back in its socket, and you clearly didn't want to. You turned quite pale. You should have got one of the stable lads to do it if it made you queasy."

"It didn't... I wasn't *queasy!*"

I gave him a disbelieving look.

"I wasn't! I've had my arm up a mare's chuff clean to the armpit to haul a foal out more times than I care to count. Think you can do something like that if you're the kind to get queasy?"

"Oh. Ew."

"I didn't want to hurt you, Gary. That was the problem. You lay there at my feet in the muck, with your hair spread out and your eyes like saucers and a face paler than usual. You told me it was all right if it hurt. And it wasn't all right. It wasn't."

Magnus held my hand pressed to his chest. I eased it free to rub over his pectoral muscle soothingly. The hair felt quite as intriguing as I'd thought it would, so I kept rubbing. "You did a bang-up job," I said. "It slid right in. First try. Barely felt a pinch."

Magnus let out a choked laugh. "Good to know."

"So you never actually had to pick me up and carry me to my bed like you did. It was my arm. My legs were fine. I could walk."

Ignoring my complaints, Magnus had scooped me off the ground and cradled me close, a big arm braced carefully at my back to avoid jostling my shoulder, and the other beneath my knees.

I was dazed from the unexpected and swift relocation from horseback to my back. I remember flailing and mumbling something about getting me a manly hurdle or a sturdy plank to stretcher me in on—*don't carry me like an infant, Magnus*—but Magnus ignored me and marched into the house.

He strode right through the Great Hall in his filthy boots and old gaiters caked with mud, which he proceeded to shed all the way up the Grand Stairs and through the house to my bedroom, bellowing for the sawbones the whole time.

He snarled at Arne when the man tried to take me off him, and he barked at the maids when they rushed up cooing. He set me down on my bed like I was made of fragile blown glass.

The only person he let near me was Mrs Robards, and

that was only because she stood her ground when he tried to run her off, too, and screeched back at him twice as loud.

If I'd known that I'd have half the household in my room, I'd have made my bed that morning with a plainer throw.

Something in a sober tweed, maybe. Or a stout plaid from the western clans my mother hailed from.

But I'd had no inkling when I set out that morning that anyone, let alone someone as overpoweringly male as Magnus would be in my room, judging it and me. So there were many, many pillows.

And the bedspread was satin.

It wasn't pink. But it was a lovely rosy apricot.

It was pink-adjacent.

More adjacent than I cared for Silverleigh's rugged stable master to ever lay eyes upon, anyway.

Or to lay *me* upon.

Slowly. Tenderly. Cupping the back of my head with his calloused hand until he slid it out from between me and my satin pillow and planted it on the mattress beside me.

For a brief moment, he'd braced himself over me in a way that was both protective and threatening at the same time, which was a bewildering mix I couldn't make sense of. He'd gazed straight down into my wide-open eyes as my breath came faster and faster.

Thankfully, I don't think he noticed the bedspread.

He hadn't looked away from me from the moment he picked me up, even when he was yelling at other people.

It was as if I was a magnet, and Magnus was...something large and made of iron.

Like a hammer. Or an anvil.

Arched over me, he'd heaved a short sigh, and he'd said the oddest thing. It was just one word. "You."

"I...what?"

Magnus gave a brittle laugh, shook his head, and then nodded it firmly. "You," he said again. It came out as a low rumble that time. A bright smile lit his face.

I smiled back helplessly and reached out with my good arm, touching my fingers tentatively to his wrist. "I what?"

"You *fucking* idiot, little brother," came from the doorway. "How can you fall off and dislocate anything at a *walk*?" Gower strolled in.

Magnus' smile vanished and he straightened, taking care not to jostle the mattress.

I remember trying to hold on, but I was too late; he stepped back and Gower pushed past him. Gower barely even seemed to notice Magnus was there, even though Magnus, at six foot five, had four inches and about fifty pounds of muscle on him.

I blushed and scowled. "It was an accident. I didn't mean to."

"You never do, do you?" Gower said. He jerked his chin at me. "You break another bone?"

"Yes."

Gower gave a tut of impatience. "You have to toughen up, Gary. When are you going to learn?"

"It was an accident."

By the time Embray had turned up to jeer as well, my cheeks were scarlet with mortification and Magnus had gone.

"That," Magnus said, his fingers tightening on where he held my ankle below the water, "was the last day I fucked a stable lad."

"Before or after I fell off?"

He shot me a look of fond exasperation. "Before, Gary. If you want to be precise about it, which I know you do, it was a few days before. My point is, no other man has been in my arms since that moment, but you."

The water had cooled around me and goosebumps pebbled my skin. Not the interesting kind that Magnus seemed to draw from me. I was just plain cold.

"That's a very long time to go without companionship for a man with such a lusty appetite," I said. My disbelief must have been obvious.

"Lusty appetite." Magnus shook his head. "Did you ever see me fucking a lad after that? Ever hear of me stepping out?"

"No."

"Ask me why, Gary."

Part of me didn't want to. I knew that whatever Magnus said next would change everything.

Then again, I was in a rapidly cooling bath, I'd started the day by being stabbed, and I had no home and no name left.

Things could change. I'd be fine with it.

"Why, Magnus?" My question came out tremblingly soft and I was about to roll my eyes at myself for being ridiculous when Magnus said, just as softly (but not trembling at all),

"Because that was the day I recognised you as my bondmate."

10

I blinked. "Right," I said. "What's that, then?"

"That, Gary, means you are the man made for me, and me alone."

I gave a nervous laugh. "Ahaha." Magnus didn't smile. "Really?"

"Really. And I am made for you. For you alone." Now he smiled. "Do you know anything about my people?"

I might have researched a bit. Actually, I'd researched a lot.

Six years ago, the old stable master, an ornery bastard called Stam who was prone to yelling and kicking at the stable cats, had died in his sleep. He hadn't been particularly good at his job, which was why no one noticed him missing for two days, and only discovered him when an unusual smell prompted someone to go looking in his chamber.

And then Magnus Torlassen came to Silverleigh.

The estate was rundown and on the brink of insolvency when he arrived, my father clinging on to the family's proud name and depending on long-gone family clout to keep the creditors from seizing everything.

Within a year, Magnus had trained and moved on nearly all of our current horses.

He traded for new stock, trained and sold them likewise, and slowly rebuilt the reputation and the coffers of Silverleigh. He'd used his contacts to make a deal that resulted in one of the kingdom's most sought-after stallions being brought over for stud.

The mares were all soon in foal, and Silverleigh's fortunes were on the up.

When the stables were under Stam's rule, I'd kept well clear, which was why my riding skills were atrocious. I knew which way to sit on a horse and that was about it.

It wasn't just stable cats and roaming dogs that Stam had liked to kick and yell at.

When Magnus was in charge, I found myself spending more and more time there, even submitting to his insistence that I must learn to ride properly, it being a disgrace that I'd reached the age of twenty-two, was of a family known for their excellent stock, and could barely stay on a horse.

I'd been fascinated by Magnus from the very start. I hadn't realised until recently—since he kissed me—that I was interested in Magnus the man rather than Magnus the intimidatingly competent horseman.

I'd researched the northern kingdom of Caithen, although there wasn't a huge amount of information on it to be found in our library. I made enquiries of the local bookseller, but she couldn't find much more.

Unlike Estla, Magnus' country didn't seem interested in jostling for continental domination or pushing its borders ever outward. It held its own borders, and minded its own business.

The opportunity to share knowledge didn't happen often, which was why I forgave myself for my somewhat lecturing tone as I sat up straight in the bath and said, "Yes, indeed I do. The horse masters of Caithen are a semi-nomadic people with seasonal camps on the steppes and established towns in the more cultivated region of the south. Their main exports are wool and grain, and they are far-renowned for their highly trained and much sought-after horses, hence being known as horse masters."

Magnus' eyes were fixed on me. His expression was open and tender.

I glanced away and trailed my hand through the water, which had turned milky and opaque with soap, and continued, "Um. It is said that a horse trained by one of the northern masters will be a faithful compan—"

I didn't get any further than that.

Magnus thrust up to his feet, catching me under the arms as he rose. He hauled me over the edge of the bath in a great wash of water, buried his hand in my hair to tug my head backward and lift my face to his.

He kissed the wits out of me.

I was panting and clutching at his shoulders when he finally tore his mouth away from mine. I hadn't even managed to bring my vision back into focus before he juggled me up into his arms, strode across the room, and flung me onto the large bed.

"Stay there." Magnus pointed at me.

Even if I did want to go anywhere, which I emphatically did not, I doubted I could get my wobbly legs to hold me up. I was shaking with excitement and arousal and, yes, a tiny amount of fear.

Magnus yanked his shirt all the way off, wrenched his breeches down, and revealed his enormous erection in all its throbbing, majestic glory. He slung a long leg over the side of the tub and stepped in, bending down for the soap.

I bit my lip on a faint squeak.

Magnus stood facing me with no self-consciousness whatsoever, and kept his burning gaze on me as he briskly soaped himself all over.

I felt my eyes grow wider and wider at the magnificent display.

Gods, he was big.

Of course, I knew that. He'd snatched me off my feet like I weighed less than a bale of hay, and tossed me. He'd had me up against a tree. He'd carried me over his shoulder. At this point, I had intimate and detailed knowledge of his size and his strength.

But...it was different with him so very, very naked.

And me.

Also very naked.

Once he'd cleaned himself thoroughly from top to toe beneath my mesmerised gaze, Magnus slowed down. The bar of well-used soap had been reduced to a thin sliver, and he worked it leisurely over his wet body, his eyes hot and on me.

I'd grown chilled as I air-dried, watching the erotic performance. I pulled the quilt from the top of the bed and wrapped it around me until only my head poked out. If I was cold, the water must be by now, too.

Magnus didn't seem to notice.

He did seem to notice where my interest lay, however.

He was very responsive to that.

Every time my breath caught—though how Magnus could hear it from all the way across the room and with the slippery, squelching noises he was making, I had no idea—he slowed down and repeated whatever had caused it.

At first this was long, slow, languorous strokes along his muscled limbs. Seeing his hard, capable hands turn sensual and light as he touched himself made my thoughts scatter.

He stroked wide circles over his pectorals and brushed his fingers over his nipples, smiling at the noise I made.

While I could certainly stand to see him do that more, it embarrassed me somehow.

I looked away, swallowing with a dry click.

When I glanced back up, Magnus had moved on and was causing rafts of bubbles to skate over his flat, tense abs. He wasn't as defined as I was there, but he was undoubtedly more muscled. He was so solid.

I held my breath when his lazily wandering hands reached his cock. To my disappointment, after a single, slow pull with a twisting motion over the head that I made a feverish note to try next time I got to touch it, his hands continued on down his body to his big thighs. Then back up.

He cupped his balls and he *lifted* them.

I thought I might simply ignite right there where I sat, and burn the whole inn down around me.

Magnus laughed out loud in delight.

Mortified, I ducked under the quilt I was wearing like a cloak. Despite him softly calling my name, I declined to come back out until I heard vigorous, businesslike splashing.

I watched Magnus finish rinsing himself off. He squeezed water from his long hair and stepped out of the tub. Grabbing a towel, he dried himself briskly if not thoroughly, and strode across the room to me.

Instead of leaping on top of me, as I had expected (I'd hoped) Magnus stood before me. His strong body was even more imposing close up.

Especially now that I had at least the *beginnings* of an understanding of what that body could do to mine.

How Magnus could lift me up, and hold me steady, and make me shiver.

I was shivering right now.

Make that quivering.

I dragged my gaze away from the large, erect cock right in front of me, a thing that I'd never expected to see at all, ever, let alone quite so close, to find Magnus watching me.

Hungrily. Patiently.

He took a deep breath and said in a strangely stilted way, "Gareth Augustus Lysander Rannock. Will you come out from under your blanket for me?"

The wording was, I thought, deliberate. Also, he used my ghastly full name, without my title, which made me think I was about to be scolded.

I chewed my lip and picked at a loose thread. "It's a quilt, actually."

He shifted and nodded, once. "Gareth Augustus Lysander Rannock," he said again. "Will you come out from under your blanket for me?"

I wasn't imagining it. There was a certain weight to his words. It wasn't just weight—the cadence was off.

More importantly, if Magnus wanted me out?

He'd pull me out.

"Does that mean something?" I asked hesitantly. "Something special?"

Magnus shifted again before replying. "Yes."

I gave him an expectant smile.

Magnus returned my gaze, his eyes narrowing.

"Well, what does it mean?" I asked when Magnus declined to elaborate.

"You know what? It's stupid. I'm being stupid. Forget about it. Come here."

I squeaked out a surprised laugh when Magnus lunged and dragged me closer. I threw myself backward, and laughed again when Magnus growled and yanked at the quilt.

"There, then," I said, and flung it away as dramatically as if it had been a playhouse villain's cape. "I am out from under my blanket. Except it's still a quilt." I couldn't help myself. "Sorry."

Magnus sucked in a deep, slow breath and his chestnut eyes sparkled. He looked so *pleased* as he set first one knee and then the other to the bed. I leaned back into my hands in an attempt to brace myself.

Magnus simply bore me down.

"Will you tell me what it means?" I said. "Please?"

Magnus' cheeks darkened as he shuffled me around until we were centred on the mattress. He fluffed a pillow, lifted my head, and set it gently down. Then he stretched out over me.

"Oof," I said on a high whistle.

Magnus grinned and took some of his weight back onto his forearms. And a little onto his knees, I suspected.

The press of his hot, naked body against mine was in equal parts alarming and thrilling.

"It's nothing," he said. "An old-fashioned tradition."

I knew a brush-off when I heard one. I kept my silence, although I couldn't do anything about my smile. He was *blushing*.

I reached up and touched his cheek in fascination.

"It's an old courting tradition," he said gruffly. "When a man or a maid finds their bondmate, especially when they're from a different clan, they sneak into the beloved's camp at night and coax them out to follow."

"Follow where?"

"Everywhere. Anywhere. Into future days. Wherever one goes, the other will follow."

"That's terribly romantic."

"It's old-fashioned." Magnus said. His tone was dismissive but his cheeks were tinged pink. "A formality most don't bother with these days. It's been a few centuries since we lived in camps. Most clans are settled now and only follow the herds during spring and summer."

"So a bondmate is like a lover? Or a...a spouse?"

"A spouse," Magnus confirmed.

"Hmm." I gazed up into his' beautiful dark eyes. Releasing his cheek with reluctance—I was enjoying that he was the one blushing for once—I reached up and traced the heavy brows, the proud nose, the divot above his top lip. Magnus tipped his head and caught my finger, playfully nipping the end. I gasped at the bright streak of sensation it caused deep in my abdomen. "And you think...you think perhaps I'm your bondmate?"

"No, Gary," Magnus said with a pitying edge.

I scowled. But he *had* said it.

"I don't think perhaps you are. I know you are." He brushed his lips over mine; a gentle nudge, the faintest touch of his tongue. "You have been. For three years."

I stared some more. The kiss was lovely.

But I felt myself beginning to squint.

"Magnus?"

"Mm?" He was still kissing me.

"Are you telling me that I'm your husband?"

His mouth curved against mine before he lifted away. "In the way of my people. Yes."

"And in your mind, according to the way of your people, we've been married for three years?"

"Yes."

I was definitely squinting at him now, and my lips were pursing. "You didn't think to mention it? At any point?"

He rubbed my disapproving pout with a thumb. "I was biding my time."

"Until *when*?" I demanded, and flung out my arms. They came to rest either side of my head.

I could tell Magnus liked it by the way his nostrils flared. My hands twitched as I fought my inclination to hide. I relaxed and deliberately uncurled my fingers.

I'd spent the last three years absolutely oblivious to the fact that this fascinating man somehow wanted me—me, *Gary*—and then he just announced that we were married?

I really felt like that was something you should *tell* a man.

I'd been dragged across the kingdom and set on the throne without anyone asking.

Now I was a husband without asking?

"I was waiting until you were ready," Magnus said patiently.

"For what?"

He flexed over me. "This."

I gasped, my neck arching.

I loved the touch of his hands on me. I thrilled at the slide of his tongue against mine.

Having his naked body drag against mine was something else altogether.

I'd never been this close to another person in my life. I felt him everywhere.

I wasn't going to let him distract me with it, though.

"I rather suspect that if you'd put your proposal to me

three years ago as compellingly as you have today, I'd have been ready then."

"No, you wouldn't," he said.

I frowned. "I would."

Boldly, I tried a little flexing of my own.

I didn't get anywhere with it, what with him being so heavy and pinning me completely, but I liked the feel of my muscles working against something so unyielding.

Magnus shook his head. "Trust me, I know how to tame a skittish creature," he said.

I laid a hand on my own chest. "Skittish creature?"

Magnus blinked slowly.

Okay, he had a point. If he'd marched up to me one day out of nowhere, and said, *I've decided we're married, now come along, spouse, time for fucking*, I'd have been more than confused.

And Magnus was an intimidating man.

So, I'd have bolted.

But still, this was all very high-handed of him.

"Do I get to accept this proposal at any time?" I asked, quite shortly for me, and I was proud of myself for it. "Or is that not for me to do? I'm supposed to go along with what you want because you want it?"

"Not because *I* want it, Gary. That's not how it works at all. Because *we* want it."

"How did you even know I wanted it without asking me?"

"You're not very subtle," he said. "Such an expressive little face as you have. If you could only see the way you look at me. How often you look at me. Thinking you're well hidden. My beloved, you have told me how you feel, over and over."

That stole my breath clean away. Sweetheart made me dizzy. *Beloved*? I vibrated with it.

Magnus raised his brows as if to say, you see?

I gaped up at him. At this beautiful, arrogant man who apparently had decided that I was the only one for him, and had denied himself and abstained from all other men for—

Wait.

"Have you seriously not been with anyone for three whole years?" I said wonderingly, struck with the realisation.

I used to watch him often. I could even accept, now, that I'd positioned myself quite deliberately in places I was most likely to come across him (the hayloft, the stable yard, the kitchens). And it had been such a long time since I saw him with another man.

Was it really three years?

Magnus nodded. "Three whole years."

"That must have been quite the ordeal," I said. "Considering how much you used to do it. Was it *all* the stable lads? Or did it just seem that way?"

His eyes glinted. "Were you tucked away spying on me all the time? Or does it just seem that way?"

"No! I wasn't spying on you! I never did it on purpose."

That was a big fat lie.

I didn't always do it on purpose.

At first.

But honestly, as I had already said once tonight, Magnus had a lusty appetite. For a while there, it had been hard to catch him when he wasn't with someone.

"Hmm," he said with amusement. "It wasn't all the stable lads. Though, it was plenty."

"And you just stopped. Because you picked me up off the cobblestones and thought, *Oho, this man of below-average height with dung in his hair and his arm hanging from the socket is the one for me?"*

"Because I held you in my arms for the first time and I knew, deep in my heart, that you were meant for me and I was meant for you." He smiled down into my face.

Oh.

"Yeah," he said, brushing the backs of his fingers over a hot cheek. "You looked at me like that."

I could only imagine that I looked like a stunned mullet.

There was no accounting for taste.

"Why would I want anyone else when you were near?" Magnus said. "How could I?"

Now I came to think of it, he had been a lot more present in my life after that day.

He'd accompanied me on rides himself rather than assigning me a stable lad. I'd stumbled upon him going about his daily business more frequently, without having to put myself in a likely location first. We chatted—awkwardly, at least on my part—where before we hadn't.

Where before, I had been one more job for Magnus. And after, Magnus had been...courting me?

Magnus shifted restlessly. I couldn't help but notice that things were getting demanding below the waist.

By which I meant that Magnus' erection was lying like a brand against my hip, and Magnus was moving against me —almost imperceptibly, but he was moving.

"Three years," I marvelled. I decided to try teasing again. "However did you manage?"

"I used my hand, Gary."

He smiled wide when I choked.

Slipping a hand between us, Magnus brought our cocks together and held them tight in his hard, work-rough palm.

"I used it a lot. And you? What did you do, while you were waiting for me?"

My neck arched when Magnus slowly, infuriatingly slowly, dragged his fist up and down. Up and down. "Oh, nothing. I'm not really...I don't usually..."

I could tell Magnus, couldn't I? That I hadn't done any of this before?

It wouldn't be too embarrassing would it?

I didn't think he would be too astonished. Obviously, he couldn't *know*. But he might have an inkling?

"I know, sweetheart," Magnus said. "You were waiting for me."

Had I been?

Before Magnus, no one had stirred even the slightest interest in me. Perhaps I was waiting for him after all.

Magnus was slowly stroking us both, his gaze attentive on my face. "One day, Gary. One day, you'll feel a fraction of what I feel for you, and you'll understand. Until then—" he lowered to kiss me and murmur against my parted lips, "—trust me."

I did trust him. More than anyone.

I loved him.

I'd spent my entire life being uncertain about many things—what to say, how to be, all the while trying to fulfil my given roles in life to the best of my ability. To be a good son, a good lord, a good king.

I had failed spectacularly on all counts.

But, when it came to Magnus, there wasn't even a drop of uncertainty.

I'd thought I was fascinated by his large, strong body and his sturdy, capable masculinity.

I'd thought that fascination was abstract and objective. Studious, even.

I'd thought that I sought him out and spied on him because he was so different from all the other men I'd ever known. That the fizzing warmth he sparked in me when I had his attention was happiness at having a powerful man look at me, for once, with approval.

I hadn't known until now that I'd taken one look at him and fallen in love.

I did trust him.

But when it came to my feelings, I didn't trust him more than I trusted myself.

Magnus knew how to make me shake and moan and come in my breeches. He called me expressive, and might well be able to read my face as easily as I read one of my books.

He couldn't possibly know how much I loved him.

In fact, I probably loved him more.

I considered him thoughtfully. It was something we could debate in the future, I decided. For now, I leaned up, kissed him, and said, "I love you, Magnus."

His slowly moving hips stuttered against mine.

I followed it with the words of *my* people, and said, "Will you marry me?"

11

Magnus' lips parted and he blinked.

He didn't say anything, though.

It wasn't quite the enthusiastic response I'd been hoping for. Okay. Words of his people, then.

"Um. Will you come out from under your blanket for me?" I tried instead.

I had about a second to feel foolish about it, and start wondering if I'd just been desperately inappropriate, before Magnus fell on me and started kissing me again.

"Yes," he groaned between kisses. "Yes, and yes, and yes."

He kissed me until I was breathless and squirming, and then he rolled us over and settled me on top.

I shuffled around up there awkwardly, intrigued by the sensation of Magnus' hot, hard cock pressing between my naked cheeks. My thighs were spread wide and I had a knee on the mattress either side of him.

It was lucky that I was so flexible; he was a big, solid man. I braced my hands on his chest.

Magnus' eyes flared. "You want to ride me?" he said, his voice low and dark.

I cocked my head. *Ride* him? "Like a...? Like a horse?"

Magnus gave a crack of laughter. "Almost. Here. Let me show you." Big hands caught my hips. He dragged me forward and then back, forward and then back.

I resisted at first, stiff and uncertain. I clutched his forearms, feeling the tendons and corded muscles flexing beneath my fingers as he moved me with ease despite my awkwardness. The arousing position and the intensity in his face caused my body to soften, to turn heavy and supple.

I fell into the rhythm he was coaxing out of me.

"Mhm," he said, the hum catching in his throat. "Just like that." His broad, flat cheekbones were flushed a deep red. So were his ears. I found it oddly charming.

I must have been equally red, although I doubted it was half as charming. A wave of prickling heat rushed over me when Magnus readjusted us and his cock began to work between my cheeks. Or more accurately when Magnus began to work me over his cock where it lay on his belly, scorching hot and hard as anything I'd ever felt.

"That...*oh*." I gasped. "Oh, that feels nice. But...oh. We shouldn't, we shouldn't. Please stop."

He did, at once, smiling up at me.

Even though I'd told him to stop, my hips continued to hitch in tiny movements. I couldn't seem to hold still. "Magnus," I said urgently. "I'm a terrible rider. I am *awful*. You know this. What if I fall off and break something?" My gaze tracked down to my hard cock, and I winced. "Or what if something pops out that really shouldn't? Both of those things have happened before."

Magnus tightened his abdominal muscles and sat up using his impressive core strength. Curving a hand around the back of my neck, he drew me close until our foreheads rested together. "I can teach you how to ride," he said. "If there's one thing I can do, it's that."

I obligingly kissed the smiling lips offered up to mine. I held the sides of Magnus' stubble-rough face and delighted in that delicious abrasion on my palms, against my own cheeks. Sighing into the sweet, drugging kisses, I whispered into his mouth, "No, you can't." I pulled back and gave him an apologetic shrug. "You haven't managed it yet. And you've been trying for six years."

Magnus met my gaze. "You have a point," he said, and made me shriek when he flipped us.

He turned me to my stomach and slid over me, angling to one side to keep his chest from pressing against my graze. "I *will* teach you," he said, whispering low and sultry in my ear. "I must. I have dreamed of it." He broke off to mouth at the nape of my neck. "I have dreamed of watching you above me, taking your pleasure."

I arched my back, pushing up against his unyielding weight as I whimpered into the pillow.

"But maybe we'll work up to it." His voice vibrated with amusement.

"It's probably the wisest course of action," I agreed wistfully.

I liked the sound of it, even though I lurched about like a sack of potatoes at anything faster than Hazlette's sedate walk. Even though the thought of bouncing around on top of Magnus made me feel horrifyingly exposed.

It was startling that the idea of being exposed to Magnus like that didn't make me want it any less.

I was beginning to think that I had heretofore unexpected depths to my character.

I could very well turn out to be a complete minx. I'd teased Magnus on purpose at least three times now.

For a long moment, I simply lay there beneath him. The novel delight I felt in having Magnus on top of me, the unfamiliar sensation of having someone so close that their body heat sank into my skin, that their heart beat against my back, slowly changed to something dark and insistent.

I squeezed my eyes shut. I flung out a hand and gripped Magnus' thigh, digging in my fingers. "Magnus," I gasped.

"Shh," Magnus said. "It's all right. I have you."

"I don't know what to do."

"You don't need to."

I squirmed up to my elbows and twisted my neck in an attempt to look him in the eye.

I had to tell him.

I'd been thinking that maybe I could get away with hiding my complete lack of experience and the fact that no one else had ever wanted me, but I just…I couldn't keep it from him.

Magnus' eyes were on me, soft and watchful. In the low light they looked darker than usual. "Do you want to turn over?" he asked.

"Oh. Yes, that'll probably be easier. For, um. Conversational purposes." I shuffled about in an effort to turn over.

Magnus was no help at all.

I was sure that he was doing it on purpose; making me rub myself all over him as I heaved and thrashed around until I was lying on my back again, gazing up at him.

"So beautiful," Magnus said. He was propped up on his forearms, head tilted as he watched me with a curious half-smile. His presence surrounded me.

I swiped a piece of hair out of my mouth. I didn't quite know what to do with my hands. I reached up and held Magnus' shoulders. Which was nice, because they were so thick and heavy—it would take more than a fall onto the cobblestones to pop one of these out, I thought, giving one an admiring pat—but it looked wrong. Like I was holding him off, or holding him back.

Which was the opposite of what I wanted.

I let my hands slide down Magnus' arms, and that was quite the sensation journey. Hot skin still slightly damp from the bath despite how much we'd wrestled around on the bedding already, coarse hair against my palms. Tendons tightening and releasing minutely in response to my touch.

Now I was getting distracted.

I clasped my hands together at my chest to stop them wandering, and cleared my throat.

"I don't know what to do because I haven't done this before," I said. "At all."

I gazed at the ceiling in silence until it grew unnerving, and then I forced myself to look at Magnus.

Magnus smiled at me.

"As in, none of it," I continued.

Magnus raised a single brow.

"None. As in...when you kissed me in the forest? That was my first kiss. And that was why the whole tongue thing—*oh*."

With a wicked look, Magnus ducked down and kissed me, sliding his tongue in quick and filthy.

Something in my stomach sparked like a bright, hot wire. I gave a soft whine when Magnus pulled back, chasing his lips.

He pushed me down gently.

"Mm," I said. "That was why I was surprised."

Magnus nodded, still watching me.

I ploughed on. "And the...your cock. It is very nice, by the way. Very big, and that alarms me, but it's the first cock I actually ever touched."

Magnus didn't say anything.

"Apart from mine," I said. "Obviously. And...this whole naked business. Is also very new."

"Gary," Magnus said when I petered out, caught by the heat simmering in his dark eyes, overwhelmed by the sheer focus of his attention. "Are you trying to tell me you're a virgin?"

"Yes."

"I know."

"How could you *possibly* know?"

"There were a few hints. Here and there."

I frowned. "Really?"

He nodded again.

"Huh. I thought I'd done a reasonably good job of hiding it. Didn't you think I was perhaps just a little inexperienced?"

"No. I thought perhaps you had never allowed anyone to touch you like you were allowing me, and I thanked the gods for the honour."

"Oh," I said. "That's pretty."

Magnus heaved a short laugh, his big body shaking against me.

I arched into it. "I thought you'd be disappointed."

I'd barely finished speaking before Magnus said, "No. No. How could I be disappointed?"

"Because I'm not going to be as good as the stable lads. I don't...I won't know how to please you."

Instead of laughing again, even though I could tell I was amusing him, Magnus hummed thoughtfully and wound an unruly lock of my hair around his finger. "It's not about being good at it," he said. "It's about intimacy. Sharing. You don't have to perform for me."

Unlike in all my riding lessons.

"So you won't be yelling, *Heels down, my lord*! And, *Trot on*! And, *Deepen your seat*!"

"I didn't say that," Magnus replied. "In fact, I may yell all of those."

I gave him a quizzical look.

Magnus shook his head ruefully. "Gary, I know you haven't done this. I want to show you everything. I don't give a toss how many partners my bedmate's had. One or a thousand. Why should I? The only thing I care about is if you like what we're doing."

"What if I don't like it?" I fidgeted. "There's a chance I might not. I've never even considered it before."

"Then we find something you do like."

I stared at him.

Magnus sighed. "Believe it or not, I don't want to do things to you that you don't enjoy."

"I *don't* believe it. You tried to make me ride Hazlette over a jump once. I told you for an hour straight before you made me do it anyway that I didn't want to and I didn't have to try jumping to know I didn't like it."

"It wasn't a jump. It was a pole, it was on the ground, and she walked over it."

"I *told* you I'd fall off, and I—"

"And you delivered on your promise." Magnus kissed me heartily. I felt the curve of his smile against my lips, and thought it was almost as good as kissing. "Why don't we give it a go? If there's anything you don't like, you can tell me. If there's anything you want, you can tell me." He tugged the lock of my hair he was playing with. "You can tell me anything."

"I'm afraid."

Magnus cupped my cheek. "Thank you," he said, rubbing his thumb gently along my cheekbone.

"But I would like to fuck you anyway."

Magnus' smile faded. "It won't be fucking between us, Gary. Fucking's for fun. It's good, healthy fun."

"So what will we be doing?"

"Making love."

"Magnus. You really are very romantic. I had no idea."

"Just you wait until we're not trying to flee the kingdom and I have all the time in the world to spend on you."

I stared at him. Then I lunged up and said between quick, pecking kisses, "No. I don't want to wait. I want...I want..."

"I know what you want."

Kissing me back, Magnus slid an arm under me, tangled our legs together, and very slowly turned us until I was draped over him. "Shh," he said when I stiffened. "I'm not going to make you ride me. I need to get you ready."

"No, you don't," I assured him. "I'm about as ready as I can stand to be." I nibbled on his lips, making him gasp. I did it again.

With a groan, Magnus pulled back long enough to pant out, "I have to prepare you."

"I'm prepared," I said confidently.

I kissed the corner of Magnus' mouth, then his jaw, then his neck. I opened my mouth over his skin. It was hot and damp against my lips. I flicked out with my tongue and tasted salt.

I'd stumbled upon Mrs Robards doing this to Arne once.

At the time, I couldn't think why she would be pulling his head back by the hair to kiss his throat, or why Arne would stand there, crowded up against his desk and clearly enjoying it—right up to the moment I'd walked in, they'd sprung apart, and everyone was shrieking and apologising at full volume until I ran away, with Mrs Robards shouting threats about sewing bells on my breeches so people could hear me coming.

Now, however, I was seeing the appeal.

And although I had no actual hands-on experience of any of this, my unfortunate talent for coming across people kissing all the time was finally paying off.

Maybe I wasn't as clueless about the whole thing as I'd thought, with a swell of confidence.

"I'm prepared," I said again, and dragged my lips over to where I could see the frantic pulse beat in Magnus' thick neck. I opened my mouth and scraped my teeth tenderly over the hot skin.

"No, Gary," Magnus said in a ragged voice. "I have to prepare you here."

His big hands had been on my arse, helping me to rock gently against him. When he said *here*, he slipped his fingers between my cheeks and touched my hole.

I bit him.

12

"Ow," Magnus said.

"Oh, no. I am *so* sorry. I... That was absolutely unintentional. I didn't mean to! You startled me! I'm so *sorry*." I soothed and patted at the patch on Magnus' throat where I could, to my shame, see the tiny indentations of my teeth.

Thank the gods I didn't break the skin.

"Gary. Gary." Magnus was speaking, but I was too appalled at myself to listen.

That was twice I'd bitten the man now.

It was going to look deliberate.

I lurched forward with a strangled shriek when Magnus pinched my buttock. Hard.

"That got your attention," Magnus said.

I glared down at him indignantly.

Magnus burst out laughing. "You look scandalised," he said.

"I am scandalised. What on earth were you doing?"

He'd *poked* my *arsehole*.

"Don't like it?"

I felt the first ripples of panic.

Was...? Was I supposed to?

"I don't know if I like it, I'm busy being scandalised you did it in the first place. Whyever would you?"

Magnus gripped my arse cheeks and held them.

That was nice. I gave him a warning look when his fingers flexed, but all he was doing was kneading gently. His fingers didn't go anywhere.

"Right," Magnus said. "All those times you saw me with the stable lads...what did you think was happening?"

"Fucking."

He contemplated me for a moment. "Tell me what that means to you, Gary."

I hadn't actually thought about the mechanics of it at any great length. Why would I? It all seemed like a lot of unnecessary heaving and thrashing about, and loud, dramatic grunting.

I really didn't care to know the details of what was going on. I didn't care that it was even going on in the first place.

Except for when I saw Magnus doing it. That always fascinated me. But then, everything Magnus did fascinated me.

Magnus jiggled my buttocks "Gary," he said patiently. "What did you think was happening?"

"I don't know, really."

"You don't know?"

I wrinkled my nose. "More like I didn't care?"

"Mm."

I stared at him. He seemed thoughtful.

I wracked my brains for what it was I was missing here.

Magnus stroked his hands slowly up to the small of my back and then down again, squeezing gently. I sighed and hitched my hips against him.

"Did your father never talk to you?"

"About...um...fucking? Sorry—making love?"

"Fucking, coupling, making love. Any of it."

I snorted. "No."

"Your brothers must have said something, surely?"

"Oh, they said lots of things. Nothing I wanted to hear, though. Awful things about the maids, and sometimes one of the footmen or gardeners. Things about me, too, like I was lucky we'd run out of funds before it was time for me to go away to school like they had because I was small and weak and I'd have been bent over all day long, and—"

Magnus growled.

I traced his heavy brows, watching my fingertip brush over the rich dark brown. I hadn't known before now how smooth and silky eyebrows could be. "I didn't listen to them," I said, distracted.

"Your mother?" he said flatly. "She never told you anything? For your eventual wedding night?"

"My mother was a very private woman, and a lady. She died when I was eight years old. It never came up."

"And you were never curious about it?" Magnus sounded a little desperate.

"No?"

"You have been very sheltered, my love." Now he sounded sad. "Very isolated."

I shrugged. "I don't feel like I've missed out on anything."

His hands tightened around my waist. "I suppose that is some comfort."

"If I was interested, I could have asked my brothers. On second thought, perhaps not. They'd have told me horrible things to frighten me." Wanting to drive away Magnus' troubled frown, I added, "I could have asked Arne."

Magnus grinned. "What a conversation *that* would have been."

I shuddered at the very thought.

Arne was younger than my father by a decade or so, but he was twice as stern and three times as imposing.

"I'm not an idiot, Magnus. I have lived in the country all my life. I've seen the beasts in the fields. And there are the horses, of course. For goodness' sake, the estate is a renowned stud. I do know how the foals are made. I know that they're not grown in the cabbage patch, despite what Nanny Haig said."

There was a reason I took particular care to avoid the stable yard on the days that stud business was being conducted.

Before Magnus came and turned things around, we hadn't bred many horses, and all they used to do was turn the mare out with the stallion and hope for the best. After Magnus, when people would send their mares to us to be covered by one of our stallions, they'd send along someone to make sure it was the stallion they'd paid an obscene amount for, and the deed was done.

I'd seen the whole process once.

Once was enough.

I'd been on my way to read in the hayloft, and maybe play with any kittens, and I'd timed it badly. My attention was drawn by the kerfuffle in the paddock, and I'd come to an abrupt and horrified halt.

A couple of lads were handling the mare in the small paddock adjoining the yard, Magnus had a halter on the prancing stallion and was handling him, and all of this was in case something 'went wrong', one of the loitering lads told me when I asked why they didn't give the horses some privacy.

I didn't even like to think about what that meant.

I stood there, mouth hanging open, transfixed as the stallion mounted an excited and squealing mare who was pressed against the fence.

His enormous unsheathed cock had gone right up in the mare, and he'd humped and thrust away as she did her best to brace herself for it.

Not unlike the way the stable lads had braced themselves over the saddle tree or up against the wall or over the manger while Magnus moved behind them, I thought now.

Although the way Magnus moved, with controlled power and deliberate rhythm, hadn't repelled me at all.

And of course, it wasn't quite the same. The lads weren't mares, and Magnus couldn't have...been inside them in any way...or...?

Because where would he put...?

"Gary?" Magnus stroked my face. "What's wrong? You've gone green."

"You're going to put it up my arse, aren't you?" I said.

"Not if the thought of it makes you go green, I'm not," Magnus said dryly.

"Is *that* what you were doing to all those lads? It is, isn't it? *Is that what everyone's been doing the whole time, and I just never knew?* People go around putting their cocks in other people's arses?"

Why would I even suspect such a thing?

Magnus' face was alight with amusement. "Depending on what they like and who they're doing it with, yes. And in their chuffs, if they have them. Sometimes their mouths."

"It wouldn't fit in my mouth, either!"

"You'd be surprised where it can fit," Magnus said, reaching up and running a thumb along my bottom lip. It was sensitive and swollen from all the kissing. "Takes practice, is all. A little preparation."

Without thinking, I licked the stroking thumb.

Magnus' eyes heated. He pressed his thumb a little more firmly to my lip. Watching my face intently the whole time, he slowly pushed it into my mouth.

I jerked my head back, startled. Magnus paused, and did it again. I held still.

"Good," Magnus said. "Now close your lips around it."

I did.

"Suck it for me."

I stared at Magnus. His brown eyes were almost black, his pupils had enlarged so much. His face had taken on that harsh, hawkish look that made me shiver.

It also, I'd come to realise, made me want to provoke him.

I did as Magnus instructed, even though I felt stupid, like a lamb at the bottle. I sucked gently.

Magnus' breath came out rough.

Intrigued, I curled my tongue around his thumb, lowered my lids, and sucked again.

His fingers spread wide along my jaw. His hips pushed up into mine and his breaths deepened. "Like that," he said, then squeezed my jaw gently and drew away.

Magnus was grinding slowly now, his hips moving in a subtle roll, working against me.

I cleared my throat. "Your cock is a lot bigger than that," I said uncertainly.

"It is."

"But you'd like it if I...?" I trailed off and cast my mind back to one of the first times I'd stumbled across Magnus. I was seeing the world in a whole new way. "Ohhhh. Was that why Harlo was on his knees that one time when I walked into the stable?"

"Yes."

"You said he'd dropped a hoof pick in the straw and was looking for it!"

Magnus stared at my mouth. "He wasn't."

"Hmm."

I thought about it.

I thought about sinking to my knees before Magnus and coming eye to eye with his manly equipment. I'd like to get a good look. It had felt so wonderful in my hand.

And I didn't think I'd ever be able to get it in my mouth, or anywhere, but...I could look at it?

Briskly, I pushed up and tried to slither down Magnus' body.

Magnus caught my elbows and hauled me back up. "Where do you think you're going?" he said.

My cheeks heated. "I was going to...you know."

"Suck my cock?"

That was a smidgen more ambition than I had, but I said bravely, "Yes."

I'd look at it first. Then I'd suck it.

"Gary?"

"Yes?"

Magnus had a rueful, heated look on his face. "I think we'll wait for that."

"We don't have to. I can do it now. I want to. I want to please you."

His intensity softened. "You have no idea how much you are pleasing me right this very moment."

"I think you mean amusing you," I said. I was shooting for tart. It came out quavery.

"I am amused at myself for all the assumptions that I

have made. You are a delight. And, my sweet delight, I am not letting your teeth anywhere near my cock until you're less likely to be surprised by new experiences. You have a terrible habit of biting when startled."

He had a very good point.

I pressed my lips together and tried not to let the grin loose.

Magnus laughed out loud, held my face and drew me down for a smacking kiss. His eyes, when he pulled away, were sparkling.

I tilted my head and smiled back, bemused.

Magnus sighed. "You are so beautiful," he said. "You could have had ten thousand lovers by now, simply by smiling their way."

Beautiful? I snorted. "I didn't want ten thousand," I said. "I didn't want any."

"Do you want me?" Magnus asked. "As a lover? You are my bondmate, Gary. It's you for me, and me for you. Whether or not we make love. That's a part of it, but not the whole. It doesn't mean you have to let me do anything to you that you don't want."

"I didn't want any lovers," I said again. "But I think, perhaps, I've always wanted you."

Magnus made a curious noise. He settled me comfortably over him again. My legs slipped to the outsides of Magnus' big thighs, and he rearranged us so that our cocks were brushing. He didn't move. He was listening.

"I didn't know what it was I wanted, though," I told him.

All I'd known was that I wanted to be close to Magnus. I wanted his approval, his smile, his attention. I liked the sound of his deep voice and his big laugh.

I ducked a little in guilt.

I liked the sound of his deep voice roughened in pleasure, even though I'd only ever allowed myself to hear one or two moans before I politely blocked my ears.

"You didn't notice me at first," I said. I traced patterns over Magnus' chest, big swooping curlicues and hearts. "If I'd smiled at you?"

"I'd have stayed far, far away."

I frowned.

Magnus pinched my chin. "I'm not stupid enough to try for a tumble with my employer's innocent young son."

I drew myself up and widened my eyes deliberately at Magnus.

Magnus widened his back.

"But you'll steal a king and drag him into your bed?" I said, voice high and snippy.

(I was a minx. I knew it.)

"Ex-king," Magnus reminded me. "And you have a title that outranks any other, in any land." He stroked my arse in lovely, smooth circles, sweeping his hands up to squeeze my waist and pull me in closer for a moment, then letting me go to stroke firmly back down again. "Bondmate."

I hitched my hips. I'd been doing it for a while, and Magnus was encouraging it. There was no urgency to it, and I kept touching Magnus' broad chest, his arms.

Any minute now, I'd work up the nerve to touch his nipples the way he had in the bath.

Or not.

Simply the thought of it made my hips jerk hard and my cheeks scorch with embarrassment again.

"I'm lying," Magnus said on a big sigh, and shook his head. His dark hair was spread out over the pillows. A strand of it was caught in his stubble.

He was lying? What were we talking about again?

"If you had so much as crooked your finger at me," he

continued, "I'd have had your breeches around your ankles and you up against the wall with your lovely thighs around my waist fast enough to make your head spin."

My stomach plunged. "That sounds exciting."

"Doesn't it?" Magnus' wandering hands went down to my 'lovely' thighs. He lifted me and shifted me with arousing ease, draping me so that our legs were now entwined.

I hissed. Oh, that was *better*. I could feel Magnus' cock much better this way. It was rigid against my belly, and thrillingly hot.

"Of course," he said, "the moment I'd tried to get close, you'd probably have bitten me."

"I'm not doing it on purpose!" I said indignantly. "You keep startling me, and frankly, Magnus, you should know better, what with being a supposedly legendary tamer of horses."

"I think I'm doing a fairly decent job of taming you."

I couldn't argue there. I was naked and writhing on top of him, after all.

Magnus wove his fingers into my hair and drew me down for a kiss.

This one was different. I wondered if all of Magnus' kisses were unique, if I'd be getting new kisses for the rest of my life. Or if I'd learn them and perfect them, one by one.

I liked both options.

This kiss was slow and sweet, with a dark promise simmering behind it.

Magnus stroked his tongue over mine, invading and retreating, encouraging and teasing me to push back, to chase him. Our lips parted softly and came together again. Magnus murmured something, adjusted the angle, and suckled softly on my bottom lip.

I bumped my hips into his hard at that, and then…I kept on bumping.

At first it was graceless, as I often was, but then I fell into a rhythm. I was suddenly aware of my own back muscles, low at my spine, tensing and releasing as I pushed my hips into Magnus' and Magnus pushed back.

Panting, I began to twist in his hold.

"Yeah," Magnus whispered, his words all but drowned in the kiss, "yes. Keep doing that. Gods, keep doing that."

I did. I held the side of Magnus' neck with one hand, and leaned some weight into the other as I braced over him and worked my hips, now in rolling thrusts, now in tight, flirtatious circles.

I watched his face anxiously, trying to gauge if I was doing it right.

"Perfect," Magnus said. His smile was fierce. "You're doing it perfectly, Gary."

I pressed against him hard and panted, my thigh muscles burning.

Magnus pulled me in again, and again, and again. Harder. Faster.

The bed creaked beneath us.

I had never imagined pleasure like it.

I hadn't spent much time imagining pleasure at all, at least this kind.

Physical pleasure had been warm soft glows, a gentle thrill in my heart. Hot buttered toast and honey cakes. Cosy blankets and a new book. Sweet tea.

I simply hadn't imagined that my body could *feel* so much. Oh, *everywhere*.

My skin was sensitised, damp with sweat as I brushed and slid over Magnus' body. I couldn't get enough of the sweetness of his mouth.

If you'd told me even yesterday that I'd have been moaning helplessly while flailing around naked on top of my former stable master, and actually trying to suck on his tongue, I'd have sat you down in the cool quiet somewhere and called for a physician.

My muscles worked in ways they never had before, even in spite of all my calisthenics. I seemed to have developed a sinuous articulation at the base of my spine and I was moving in a whole new way, languid and powerful, all to help me slide and glide over Magnus, seek out the best parts of his body—the parts that I could rub against, that gave me delightful slippery friction against my cock.

The parts that made Magnus gasp and thrust back harder.

I felt securely located inside my body, inhabiting it in a way I never had before. It was terrifying. It was wonderful. I was utterly undone and completely safe at the same time.

This must be what the horses feel like, I thought nonsensically, when Magnus lets them gallop across the fields beneath him.

I tore my mouth free, light-headed and panting for air.

Magnus growled and rolled us. Oh yes, better, better. I wrapped my legs around his hips.

"Your wound," he gasped. "Is it—"

"No, it's fine. It's fine. It's a graze. I can't feel it, I don't care. Please don't stop."

Magnus planted his hands either side of my ribs. He lifted away so he wasn't rubbing my back over the sheets, and we both moaned helplessly at the changed angle. He slid his knees wider and drove his thrusts down hard against my pelvis.

I held on to his muscled sides, staring up at him in wonder.

He looked truly wild.

His hair was damp and mussed, his eyes were burning, his teeth were bared. If he'd looked at me like that before this very moment, I would have have screamed and run away.

Instead of taking it in, revelling in the evidence of what I was doing to him, of how we were building this astonishing thing between us and then, oh—Magnus scooped a hand beneath me, grasped a buttock and lifted me, aligning our cocks in a way that was so perfect it sparked sensation over me from my scalp in a shivering rush all the way down.

Magnus worked against me, relentless.

My spine arched suddenly, snapping tight.

My shoulders dug into the mattress as my chest and neck bowed. I cried out again and again as Magnus held me close and ground in. Heat bloomed between us.

After I'd finished crying out in a soft, broken voice I didn't even recognise, and my quivering taut muscles unlocked and let me sink back into the pillows, I blinked up at Magnus in time to see his beloved face twist. He moaned with a long, shuddering sigh that raised the hairs on my arms.

He relaxed onto me. More like collapsed, actually.

"Oh, gods," I said. "Can't breathe."

"Sorry." Magnus shot me an apologetic smile and slid off to the side, bringing me with him. He fussed us about until he had one heavy thigh slung over my legs and an arm around my waist.

It was a good thing I didn't have any compelling urge to put some space between us, because I was clearly going nowhere.

I had the opposite urge, in fact. I shuffled closer and tucked my head against Magnus' throat, under his chin.

Magnus chuckled and stroked the back of my hot neck.

When my heart had stopped thundering, I yawned and said, "So when is the part when you put it in my arse?"

There was a surprised silence, and then he burst out laughing again, holding me close. "Not tonight, that's for sure. For one thing, I have a decade and change on you, and I can't recover that quickly from coming that hard. For another, I never planned on taking you that way tonight. Once again, I got carried away." He tipped my face to his and kissed my nose. "We've got at least five days of hard and fast travel ahead of us, Gary. That makes it the worst time in the world to be getting inside you for the first time."

I blinked up at him. "Why?"

"You'll be sore."

I wasn't quick enough to hide my grimace. I *knew* it was going to hurt.

His arms tightened around me. "I said you'd be sore, not in pain. I won't ever hurt you."

I shifted, rubbing against him. Even spent, his cock was an alarming size and an even more alarming thought with regards to it entering me. "I don't see how you can avoid it."

"I know a few tricks."

His hand glided over my arse. I bucked my hips into his again. Slowly, he slipped his fingers between my cheeks. I stiffened.

"What I'll do," he said in a conversational tone, "is get you used to it nice and slowly." He brushed lightly over my hole. "Like this. Soft and sweet. With a little something to ease the way." He kept doing it.

My breathing picked up. "Something like what?"

"Oil."

"I'm not sure I like the sound of that."

"Then I'll gentle you another way. I'll start by kissing you there instead."

I straight-armed myself away from his chest and stared up into his face, feeling my eyes stretch wide. "Whaaat?"

He grinned at me.

"You wouldn't," I said.

"Hmm." His eyes glinted. "We'll have to see, won't we?" He stopped touching me, and swatted my buttock. "That's for later. When we're safe and settled. For now, sleep."

Sleep?

After *that* comment?

"And, Gary?" Magnus said.

I was boggling at the thought of him kissing me right there. I couldn't quite picture how that would go. I'd have to be spread-eagled on my front for it, wouldn't I? Or maybe—

"Gary?" Magnus leaned down and kissed me quickly, a demanding press to get my attention.

I chased after his lips and was disappointed when he kept himself out of reach. "Yes?"

"You know that I won't ever do a thing to you that you don't want, don't you?"

"Yes, of course." I smiled up at him. He held me tight and I softened against him, yawning again.

"Sleep," he said. "You're safe."

I hummed into his throat, my eyes closing.

He kissed the top of my head. "I have you."

13

It was morning when I woke up—not quite dawn, but early. I blinked my heavy eyes open as my thoughts drifted.

The light in the room was soft and pearly grey. Sun spilled through the uncurtained window to lie on the quilt and warm the side of my face.

A year ago, I'd have been at home, blissfully unaware of the political turmoil poised to snatch me up in its jaws, chew me up and spit me out.

My bedroom at Silverleigh was large and comfortable. I used to lie in bed, surrounded by mounds of pillows that I could nestle among, and snuggled beneath a deliciously heavy satin coverlet with fanciful embroidery that I would idly run my fingertips over.

In spring and summer, the ivy on the walls outside my window shivered with restless activity when house sparrows were building nests and raising young. Beyond the chatter of the sparrows, I'd hear doves cooing in the dovecote in the herb garden, or perhaps the crows and jackdaws in the trees a little further out, or pheasants calling in the wood.

A day ago, I was at the Palace.

My bedroom there had been enormous, cold, silent, and filled with the property of dead kings. I'd been related to every last one of them. And as far as the kingdom was concerned, I was the very last one of them.

Today, I had no idea where I was.

If you were to show me a map, I couldn't point it out.

I didn't care. It didn't matter where I was, because I did know *who* I was.

And it wasn't Gary of a Hundred Days, either.

I was Magnus Torlassen's bondmate.

He was mine.

Magnus.

I sat up sharply.

He was lounging by the fire, a small folding table laden with food before him.

The table must have been delivered along with breakfast, because it hadn't been there the night before.

Magnus had speared a large chunk of bread with a long-handled toasting fork and was holding it toward the flames. The air was scented with toast, coffee, and bacon.

Even though he had woken me last night after a short nap to eat the cold soup with bread and cheese, I was ravenous. My stomach groaned.

At my sudden movement, Magnus glanced over.

I froze.

The air brushed cool over my bare chest. I looked down, then up at Magnus, then I crossed my arms over my chest.

Then I uncrossed them, reached down, grabbed fistfuls of the quilt, and dragged it up to my chin.

Magnus watched my performance with a tiny curl at the side of his mouth, and warmth in his dark eyes. "Morning," he said.

I croaked at him. "G-good morning."

Magnus reached for a pitcher. He poured out a tumbler of what looked like apple juice, and brought it over to the bed. He sat on the edge of the mattress, his weight making me lurch toward him, and brushed my hair back off my face.

I reached for the juice. I assumed that was why Magnus had come over.

Magnus pulled the glass back and waited for me to look at him before he tapped his own smiling lips.

Eyes on Magnus', I leaned forward and pecked a kiss on his lips.

"Thank you," Magnus said.

"Thank *you*," I said.

He gave me the juice. I took a delicate sip, watching him over the rim of the glass. I hadn't realised how thirsty I was until the fresh, sweet liquid all but sizzled as it filled my parched mouth.

I tossed any half-baked idea of drinking it in a seductive manner out the window, and drank it greedily.

"Thought you might need that," Magnus said. "Dry throat?"

Yes. Probably from all the moaning and gasping I'd done the night before.

I blushed and nodded.

"Not surprised," Magnus said. "You snore like a hog."

He ruffled my hair and strode back to the fire where he threw himself into the seat.

My mouth dropped open. A *hog*? "I do not!"

Magnus shovelled in a heaped forkful of bacon, and before he'd even chewed it, he stuffed in a great quivering load of what looked like griddle cakes, dripping with honey. He nodded. "I had no idea. Quite the eye-opener, it was. A refined lordling such as yourself, sprawled out on your back, mouth open and catching flies, snoring fit to break the barn."

I snapped my mouth shut. "I...I do not snore!" I tossed back the covers and marched over.

Magnus pushed his chair back from the table and angled toward me, ready to receive me as I pushed my way between his legs.

"I think I'd know if I snored," I said crossly, glaring down at him.

"How could you know?" Magnus put his fork on his plate with a clink, and cupped the backs of my thighs, tugging me forward an inch. "You're asleep."

He had a valid point. "But like a hog? You mean like a sweet little piglet, don't you?" Not exactly alluring. Better than a hog.

Magnus tugged me even closer. I swayed and put my hands on his shoulders. He propped his chin on my abdominals, his stubble rasping against my skin, and grinned up at me. "You, my beloved, snore like a drunken boar." He pressed a sucking kiss to my navel that had my muscles jumping in response, and pushed me back by the hips. "Now eat your breakfast."

I was about to snippily inform him that I wasn't hungry —a whopper of a lie—when Magnus added, "Feel free to stay naked. I like something pretty to look at while I'm eating my porridge."

Gasping, I whirled around and bolted back to the bed.

I'd strutted over there in all my glory without even thinking about it.

I *was* a minx.

A bashful minx, though. I snatched up the quilt and wrapped it around me. "Where are my clothes?" I said quietly, doing a better job of hiding my nudity than my smile.

Magnus gestured over to the alcove where a stack of clothes was piled up on a stool, with a familiar pair of sturdy boots tucked beneath. I went over and stood staring down.

"These are my clothes," I said wonderingly. "*My* clothes. Did you bring them with you?"

"Yes."

While I had a weakness for pretty things and interesting textures around me, I didn't like to wear them. The royal garments had been tight and elaborate, padded and gaudy.

I'd loathed them.

I picked up one of my very own shirts off the pile. It was larger than was fashionable, but that was how I liked it. It was a plain linen, bleached and washed to a soft white and decorated at the neck and wrists with dainty embroidery that matched the colour of the fabric. It was subtle enough not to stand out and draw attention, but I knew it was there.

Bunching it up, I lifted it to my nose and inhaled.

It smelled like the linen closet. Like home.

My eyes filled with a rush of heat and I blinked rapidly.

Like the past.

Like everything I'd lost.

I cleared my throat, dragged the shirt over my head and buttoned it up to the throat. It hung comfortably loose and reached to the very top of my thighs. I contemplated my plain brown breeches and worsted stockings.

Instead of pulling them on, I folded my sleeves back to my elbows and returned to Magnus.

I hovered at his shoulder for all of a heartbeat before he slung an arm around my hips and drew me down to sit on his lap.

I sighed and melted against him.

Magnus arranged me to his liking, settled one large hand on my thigh, and with the other he dragged a bowl of steaming porridge across the table and passed it to me.

I dug in. After the first mouthful I added three teaspoons of honey, making Magnus laugh at me. We sat in silence as we ate.

How had it come to this, I wondered?

Yesterday I was staggering around in the mud and the rain, a man on the run with nowhere to go.

Now here I was, perched on my stable master's—my bondmate's—knee, half dressed, and...okay, still with nowhere to go.

But not worrying about it.

I finished my porridge, drank another glass of juice, gave Magnus my bacon because if I snored like a hog I suddenly felt repelled at the thought of eating one, and let my thoughts return to their gentle morning drifting as I gazed into the fire.

After a peaceful few minutes, during which Magnus cleared every plate on the table, and during which I very nobly didn't point out that I might snore like a hog but Magnus had the appetite of one, Magnus turned me in his arms until I was straddling his lap.

I shivered at the brush of his breeches against my sensitive inner thighs.

He ran his hands slowly up and down my back as we gazed at each other.

"What happens next?" I asked reluctantly.

If I had my way, I'd barricade the door and stay here for the next four or five decades, hiding away with Magnus.

But I knew we couldn't do that.

We'd die of dehydration within three days.

"Well, now," Magnus said. "That's up to you."

I found that very hard to believe. Nothing had been up to me. Not ever.

"When I ran from the Palace and then the city, I was just trying to stay alive. I seized the moment. I haven't had time to think beyond that. I suppose I intended to head home, but I'm not sure if...? Magnus." I shifted on his lap. "Is Silverleigh still mine?"

Magnus' hands tightened on my hips. "No, love. When they took you away, they took the estate. Installed another lord while the dust from your carriage was hanging in the air."

"Those utter tosspots," I said after a blank silence. "*Honestly*."

Magnus burst out laughing.

I chuckled along with him. "I mean, for goodness' sake. Why didn't they knock on the front door, get shown into the parlour, and put an arrow between my eyes right away? Why bother with all that nonsense of the coronation and then the attempts to kill me, and then the coup?"

"Because it's easy as anything to get away with evil if you make sure it looks like you're doing good," Magnus said. "The best way to get yourself in power is to make people think it's what they asked for. What they need."

I huffed. "It's all been such a pointless waste of time. I told them no. Why didn't they leave me be?"

"Like it or not—and this goes for you and them—it was your right to take the throne. It still is. Which Drusan and his co-conspirators all know very well. It's why they had to find a body to burn right quick, soon as they discovered you'd gone." His expression turned fierce. "I'd like to have seen them flap around when they found out. It was a canny move, though. I'll give Drusan credit for that much. If you were ever to show up and demand your throne back, they'll cry pretender. A lookalike peasant, an imposter found by rival factions, a puppet trained to mimic the king."

A puppet would undoubtedly do a better job of it than me. I never got a lick of training.

I shuddered. "I will not be showing up again, and I don't think it's my throne at all, just because I was the last man standing. I haven't the first clue about politics or ruling a kingdom or anything of the sort. And Magnus, I like learning things, but I am *not* interested in learning politics."

Magnus smiled. "If you change your mind and want the throne, I'll put you there," he said matter-of-factly.

I couldn't tell if he was joking. "That's sweet. And I have no idea how you'd even begin to manage it. But no. Thank you."

"I have ways and means."

The same sort of ways and means that had him in the city watching over me and foiling all of Drusan's plans for a hundred days straight, I suspected. "I have no ways, no means, and no taste for being in charge."

For some reason, this made Magnus' eyes darken. "You don't say," he murmured, and tugged me down for a kiss.

He palmed the back of my neck and squeezed lightly. I went boneless and gasped against his smiling mouth. As soon as my lips parted, he tilted my head with a light touch to my jaw, and stroked his tongue inside.

Still not used to it, but very much in favour, I jolted with surprise before eagerly responding.

"Mm," I said, somewhat dazed, when he released me after a slow and thorough kiss. "I *do* say. I know it's hard to believe."

He shook beneath me.

"It's true! I never even liked asking the servants to do things. Imagine how much I would hate telling a whole country to do things. I mean, they all think I did, of course. All those terrible proclamations and policies and whatnot that Drusan issued in my name to besmirch my reputation. And the tax! But no, thank you. Being responsible for a country is not something that I would willingly take on." I sighed. "I have no ways, no means. No money. No house. Nothing."

"Eh," Magnus said.

I hooked my arm around his neck for balance so that I could lean back and look into his face.

Magnus jostled me affectionately. "You have plenty of money."

"I don't see how?"

"For one thing, I stole all your horses."

"You...what?"

"Stole your horses. The whole stable. Shipped them north. Near all of Silverleigh's worth was in the horses, Gary. Especially mine, the ones I trained and bred."

There was no modesty there, and there didn't need to be. Magnus was the best. People came from other kingdoms to buy a horse he'd bred and trained.

Even for the ones he'd just trained, they'd come thousands of miles.

"You can sell them if you want, and use the money to settle. Or keep them and set up your own stables. I sent Hazlette up there, too, of course."

I pressed my lips together and my eyes dampened.

"As for the house and goods, well. Me and the rest of the servants stripped that clean."

"Oh, I am glad," I said. "You all deserve it, frankly, having had such a shocking run of masters." I patted Magnus' chest. "Good for you."

Magnus stared at me. "For *you*," he said slowly. "We

stripped it for you, Gary. Arne's holding it over the border in a few wagons. There's more than enough to get you situated comfortably and living like you're used to."

"Why on earth would they keep it for me and not...I don't know. Strike out and set themselves up comfortably?"

"Because, my beloved, unlike the rest of the idiots in Estla, who believe everything they're told, and cheer and boo when prompted like a rowdy audience at the playhouse, folk from the estate know you. Most of them watched you grow up. They're not going to steal from you."

"I wish they had," I said crisply.

Magnus arched a brow.

I hunched in a little. "Because now of course I have to give it to them and I am terrible at gift-giving. Magnus, it makes me so *anxious*."

"I know."

I gave him a questioning look.

"Last Yule," he said, and touched his jaw meaningfully.

I winced.

I'd been giving the servants gifts for Yule every year since my mother died. At least, bar the first one. It was the thing to do, and when I found out my father didn't care about it, I took it on.

I loved buying the gifts. I simply hated handing them over. I wasn't a benevolent and elegant lady like my mother. I wasn't the lord then. It wasn't really my place.

So I sort of...left the gifts lying around where the servants would find them.

Arne's in his office, Mrs Robards and Elayne's in the still-room, Jafray's and the other gardeners in the dormitory, Milar's in the sewing room and so on.

The previous Yule, Magnus had caught me trying to slip into his room and leave his present.

Thinking he was out supervising the morning exercise, I'd walked on in and seen him hauling his breeches up over his naked arse.

He'd turned to look at me, chest broad and just as naked as his arse had been.

I'd panicked.

I'd hurled his gift at him, and bolted.

Last thing I saw was his astonished face as a pair of fine leather gaiters with shining buckles smacked him right in the mouth.

"Sorry," I said, and stroked his jaw tenderly.

Magnus kissed me. "We're five days walk from the border. Three days, if I steal us horses. Which," he added at my scandalised gasp, "I won't do because some of us have morals. Not me, but that's fine. We'll stay overnight in another inn out of the way. Drusan will have his hands far too full to send anyone after you. He's probably already murdered anyone who knows you're gone anyway. To all intents and purposes, you're a ghost." He ran a hand up my inner thigh, making me lurch, and then he tweaked my bollocks and continued talking as if nothing had happened. "Once we're across the border and safe in Caithen, we'll meet up with Arne. You can distribute the wealth as you see fit. After that, I'll take you home."

I flexed my spine to rock into his hand. He tightened his grip but to my disappointment that was all he did. "Your home?" I said breathlessly.

"No."

I squirmed when Magnus tickled my knee, then gasped when that hand went back under my shirt.

Well, it was about time. I had come over here and sat on the man bare-arsed for a reason, and it wasn't because I was too warm for my breeches.

Magnus cradled my bollocks in a large, rough palm.

And that was it.

He just held them.

"Our home?" I said.

Magnus' full lips curved in a blinding smile.

"*Our* home," I said with confidence. "Wherever that is. Where is that, again?"

"It's at the very heart of Caithen. I have a small property there. Grasslands, mountains. Space as far as you can see. You'll love it. You can run forever. I've horses to train and breed. While I'm doing that, you'll have a library and a garden to build from scratch. And we have a lifetime to spend together."

I'd never heard anything so perfect in my whole life.

"I'll help you with the horses," I said.

I hadn't had much time to think about the reality of what Magnus had been doing for the three months we were in the city, but it had struck me that bribing people and paying them to stop me from being murdered was a costly business, and some of those deals Magnus mentioned he'd made would no doubt involve his particular skillset.

"You can teach me everything you know."

"Hmm?" Magnus said with interest. His large hand massaged my bollocks gently, then shifted to hold my cock.

I flexed again, pushing against him with a demanding hitch of my hips. I wanted him to do more than hold it.

If I wanted it held, I could manage that myself.

"Teach me everything you know about *horses*," I said snippily, reaching down to pluck his hand away. Only he didn't let go. He squeezed warningly. Fine. "Instead of being called Gary of a Hundred Days, the Tyrant King, I'll become Gary, the Greatest Horse Breeder and Trainer Ever Known."

Magnus' eyebrows went up and his cheek creased with that dimple.

"Right." I patted him. "Second greatest. Sorry."

Magnus sighed. "That seems unlikely."

Aim lower. All right. "Then I shall become Gary, the Greatest Rider of Horses," I stated instead.

Again Magnus tipped his head consideringly. He shook it.

"I shall be known as Gary, Bondmate of Magnus." I cupped his face and kissed him softly. "The happiest man in all the lands."

"Now that sounds likely indeed."

EPILOGUE

A hundred days later, Gary, Bondmate of Magnus, the happiest man in all the lands, was yelling at the top of his lungs.

At me, Magnus, Bondmate of Gary, the most patient man in all the lands.

"It's your fault for telling me I snore like a hog in the first place!" Gary stood in front of the pigsty with his feet planted on the rutted ground, arms spread wide, and a determined look on his face. "I have fellow feeling for them now. I've watched them sleep in the sun. I've heard them snore, which is *adorable*, by the way. Would you eat me for breakfast, Magnus? *Would you?*"

"I did just yesterday, if I recall."

Gary flushed scarlet and looked around guiltily.

There was no one to hear.

Our large but modest house sat at the foot of the mountain and gazed out over the endless steppes and into forever. You could see anyone coming from miles away, and the only other people around were Arne and Ingrid Robards.

At four o'clock in the afternoon, Arne and Ingrid were

busy doing their own thing. Together, in their own private rooms, safely tucked away where Gary wouldn't wander in on them.

I bit back my smile. "Gary," I said cajolingly.

"No. *No!*" Gary bent down and scooped up as many of the squirming pink and grey piglets as he could juggle.

Then he ran.

He hadn't taken the news that the litter would be heading to market once they were weaned at all well.

I stuffed my hands in my pockets, rocked back on my heels, and watched.

Where did he even think he was going?

He was barefoot, his legs were pumping, he was hunched over his armful of excitedly squealing piglets, and any minute now he would drop one.

Then he'd drop the rest.

And then I'd spend the whole afternoon trying to get them back in the pen, with Gary being his usual level of helpful.

Which was to say, sweetly well-intentioned, but undoubtedly making things worse.

I might as well give in now.

"Gary," I bellowed, rolling my eyes at myself. I followed up with the promise Gary had been attempting to wheedle out of me for the last ten minutes, using all sorts of sexual favours. "I promise I won't sell any of the piglets except as dear little pets."

I was going to be stuck with five useless pigs. No one ever kept a pig for a pet. Not here in the plains, anyway.

Except Gary.

I sighed.

Except me. For Gary.

He stopped and turned. His wide, silvery eyes met mine

across the distance. He was startlingly fast and had already covered a fair bit of ground, so I was too far away to see the colour. But I knew it, intimately.

I had gazed down into those eyes when they were soft with love, dark and hazy with desire, lost in pleasure, and—perhaps my favourite—just plain happy.

Gods, how I loved that man.

He had five tiny piglets in his arms. He'd always favoured overlarge clothing, preferring shirts that hung loose and easy on his lean frame. These days, he favoured *my* shirts, and he quite brazenly stole them from me.

The one he was wearing today had come untucked from his breeches at one side and was snapping in the harsh spring breeze you got in my homeland, that danced across the plains and made the long grass ripple like silver and gold water. His white-blond hair, growing down to his shoulders, streamed out behind him.

Gary had shyly told me that he wanted to grow it as long as mine. Or, perhaps, longer? I'd told him he could grow it down to his pretty arse or have Ingrid shear it to his scalp, whichever pleased him best.

There was a large part of Gary that was used to doing as he was told and not as he wanted, always trying his best to meet the expectations of others.

I was more than happy to spend the rest of my life showing him that he didn't need permission to do a damn thing, or ever wait to be told what to do.

Except in bed.

Gary very, very much liked to be told what to do in bed.

Once he got over his playfully exaggerated shock and not-so-secret delight at whatever new thing I wanted from him, he'd eagerly comply. Then he'd get crafty and test out his newly discovered power over me.

Or, he thought he was being crafty. He had no idea how open he was.

And he had no idea of how deep and all-consuming the power he held over me was.

I would, after all, do anything for him.

I stole horses and ransacked a noble's estate. I crossed the kingdom. I bribed people, threatened them, made deals, made promises I still had to deliver on.

I raged, plotted, and schemed.

I absconded with a king, spirited him away, built him a house, built him a life, and gave him my devotion.

My heart.

Making myself a laughingstock by keeping pigs as pets was nothing.

"I'll hold you to that," Gary called, grabbed for a squirming piglet, then swore and sat sharply.

The littler fuckers scattered, heading straight back to the sty and their mother, who had been snoozing, unconcerned, in the mud the whole time.

Gary looked up from the ground when I came to stand before him. His nose was a little sunburnt and his lips were chapped. "Hello," he said, and scrambled to his knees.

I shook my head. "Gary, Defender of Piglets."

Gary had the grace to look a little guilty, but still somewhat defiant.

I loved it.

"Come on." I held out a hand. "You get to keep your pigs. That means you have to hold up your end of the bargain. You're supposed to be riding me until I come so hard that I black out."

"Oh my gods," Gary hissed. "*Lower your voice.*"

"There's no one to hear."

Gary smacked the dirt off his arse and his knees fussily.

"And if I recall correctly, which I do, I said that I would ride you until you swooned in ecstasy as you reached completion."

"Same thing," I said, grabbing Gary's hand. "Let's go."

Gary pretended reluctance. It wasn't at all convincing, mostly because after three strides, he was in the lead and towing me after him.

"Because I am a wonderful bondmate and husband," I said, leaning back to make him grunt with determination and pull harder, "I'll even let you do some stretches before we start. It might take some time for that ecstatic completion to...hmm. How did you put it again? Ah, yes. To clasp me in its velvet grip. You should probably get nice and limber first. Get those lovely muscles of yours all warmed up."

Gary's hand spasmed in mine. "Now you're making fun."

"Absolutely not. I assure you, it's going to take hours," I said. "I don't care how many times you fall off. I want that velvet clasping."

His shoulders heaved as he held back a laugh.

Even when we first began a physical relationship, I'd had a fair idea of how to drive Gary wild.

After three months and a lot of practice, I was a master at it.

One of my favourite things to do was to drag our lovemaking out over a whole afternoon, until Gary was sprawled over me, limp and beaming with satisfaction.

Once we'd finished, that is.

During, he'd be pulling my hair and crawling all over me, making demands that swung from imperious to seductive to just plain Gary.

Awkward, shy, whole-hearted. Dear.

"And then after that, of course, there was talk of other things," I said.

Gary was staring at me, wide-eyed and still trying not to laugh.

"Let me see if I can remember them. Ah yes, there was you sucking my cock. And then you were going to erotically bathe me. There was something about bubbles. And then you were going to get in the bath with me for more sucking of my cock. Then, I believe—I know you'll correct me if I'm wrong here—you said you were going to get on your belly for me and hold onto the headboard and not say a word while I took my time with you and—"

"Oh, dear," Gary said, and stuck his lower lip out in a sassy pout. "You must be confused. I wasn't promising all of those things in exchange for the piglets." He walked backward, swinging my hand cheerfully. "It was a list of options. I meant you could pick one."

I laughed. "We'll see," I said.

And we did.

∼

ONCE, AS HE LAY ON MY CHEST IN THE WEAK, DAWNING sunlight, Gary had asked me if he'd ever get used to kissing. If there was a finite number of the types of kisses and if he could master them with practice, or if each kiss was always new, and he'd learn them for the first time every time.

I liked his whimsical idea of eternally new kisses, but I'd answered the former. Mostly because when he'd asked, Gary was uncertain about physical intimacy. I thought he'd feel more confident at the idea there was something to learn, a skill he could acquire.

He'd seemed thoughtful and relieved at my answer.

The truth was, every kiss with Gary was like my first kiss.

I thought I knew, before I even set out to reclaim him from those who'd stolen him from me and put him on the throne, the depth of my love for this man.

But with each kiss he gave me and every day we passed together, my love for him grew deeper, and deeper, and deeper still.

I was never going to stop falling for Gary. For the rest of my life, and whatever came after.

END

ALSO BY ISABEL MURRAY

Romantic Comedy

Not That Complicated

Not That Impossible

Worth the Wait

Merman Romance

Catch and Release

CATCH AND RELEASE EXCERPT

Catch and Release
Chapter One

"The fuck is it?" Jerry said.

I shrugged. The mystery lump that had caught his attention lay two hundred feet from where we stood on the beach. A semi-solid curtain of driving rain hung between it and us. If he couldn't see what it was, how was I supposed to?

"Come on," he said, and bustled off.

Jerry Barnes was fifty-eight years old. He'd lived every single one of those years in a little harbour town tucked away in a fold of land between Scotland and England, and yet the man still got excited by every seaweed-wrapped heap of driftwood that was coughed up by the tide.

"Joe!" he said, prancing ahead in his bright yellow wellies. "Come on!"

Seriously. He had twenty years on me, and he moved like I had twenty on him.

I couldn't conjure that amount of energy and enthusiasm even five coffees into my morning.

Especially not for something that was bound to be either boring or disgusting, depending on how dead it was, and how long it had been that way.

I followed him, but only because Jerry was still carrying my tackle box.

Since I'd moved to Lynwick six years ago, I'd built myself quite the reputation. I was well-known around these parts for being the worst fisherman to cast a line on the east coast. For some unfathomable reason, Jerry took it as a personal challenge.

Jerry owned and operated a mid-size trawler, the *Mary Jane*, with his brothers. That morning, he'd spotted me on his way home from the harbour. As usual when I didn't see him first and have time for evasive manoeuvres, he came rushing over to impart the wisdom of his family's many, many generations of fishermen.

This morning's pearl had been, "Only thing you're gonna catch if you try casting in this wind is yourself, Joe."

I was well aware. It had already taken me half an hour of fumbling with numb fingers and rapidly vanishing patience to detach the hook from the seat of my trousers.

I wasn't a complete idiot. The weather had been *fine* when I started.

Jerry had helpfully collapsed my rod and packed it away for me, even though I hadn't actually agreed to stop fishing. He let me have the rod back and hefted up my tackle box before I could grab it. I had the sinking feeling that he was about to do something awkward, like offer me lessons again, when he was distracted.

Though the tide was high, it was on the turn. Sullen waves

sucked back toward the horizon, hissing angrily under a dark metal sky. A distant liner slid ominously along the skyline, heading for Norway, or America, or maybe Antarctica. I didn't see Jerry reach the tangled mass that had been abandoned by last night's storm but when I glanced over at him, he was motionless, frizzy ginger hair whipping about his head.

I hesitated at this un-Jerry-like lack of animation.

"Well?" I called. "What is it?"

Jerry flapped his arms in an oddly helpless gesture. If he gave any answer, it was lost to the wind.

"What?" I shouted.

He turned to face me. His stone-green eyes were wide and his bushy eyebrows were halfway up his craggy forehead. An expression of excited guilt sat queasily on his face. "It's a body!" he yelled after a brief pause.

"Of what? Not a dolphin?" It was big enough and then some. This close, I could see that the large mass had been all but cocooned in a knotted and tangled monofilament net.

"Noooo," Jerry said as I came to stand beside him.

I dropped my fishing rod alongside the tackle box. "Oh, shit."

It was a man.

A pale, pale man. His skin was the fairest I'd ever seen. Who knew how long he'd been in the water? Although, there was no obvious bloat. Nothing was sloughing off. Maybe he was naturally pale?

He was big, even prone and half curled. One leg lay straight; the other was hitched up protectively into his body. He lay on his side. A thickly muscled right arm covered his head and obscured his face. His left arm was tucked beneath him.

"His hair's blue," Jerry said, and flipped a lock of it with the toe of his boot, like he was turning shells. "Really blue."

I nudged him, hard.

"Ow," Jerry said.

"Don't be disrespectful."

"He's dead, mate. Think he cares?"

"I know *I* do."

Jerry sleeved scattered seawater and rain from his face. "Reckon he's one of them club kids, then?"

I frowned. "Club kids?"

"Yeah." Jerry flailed his hands in the air around his head and whooped.

I stared at him.

"Dancers," he said. "Dancey clubs. Raves. You ever been to one?"

"Have *you*?"

"Nah. I'd feel a right prat, going into one o' them places. Used to want to, though. Back in the day." He sighed wistfully. "Never did get around to it. Think I missed the boat on that one. So. You reckon? Club kid?"

"...because his hair is blue?"

Sometimes, I struggled to follow Jerry's train of thought. I hadn't decided if our communication misfires were a generational thing, a local thing, or a Jerry thing.

Jerry grunted.

Blue hair wasn't all that unusual, even around here. Neither was pink, purple, or green. I didn't know why it said alternative club lifestyle to Jerry. The sixtysomething librarian in the next town over, which was twice the size of Lynwick and had a permanent library rather than a retro-fitted bus full of books that parked outside the pub once a week, had hair that she dyed an extraordinarily fake flat green. She wore it in a beehive. I thought it looked kind of amazing. Extra amazing when she shoved pencils in there.

The body's hair was also amazing, but nothing about it looked fake. It shone in a dark, wet snarl of indigo and cobalt, lying in long, thick ropes over his upper chest and face.

"Big 'un, isn't he?" Jerry said. "I'm thinking six four? Six five?"

"Yeah. Easy." He was closer to seven feet than six. I gazed down at him. "Who do you think he is?"

"He's not local, I can tell you that." Jerry squatted to pull at the net entangling the man. "There's no one around these parts the size of him." Jerry tipped his head to one side and paused thoughtfully. "Got a nice arse, though," he said.

I did a slow pan and gaped at him. So far as I knew, Jerry was straight.

So far as his *wife* knew, Jerry was straight.

He nodded at me encouragingly. "Right?"

I scanned the man without meaning to. A pale gleam of wet, white buttock peeked out through the holes in the net. Okay, yes. He had a nice arse.

For a corpse.

"Even I want to slap it." Jerry bent down.

I snagged him by the back of his collar and hauled him up. "Jerry, don't you dare get bi-curious and start slapping a dead man's arse."

Jerry batted my hands away. "Holy shit," he said. "Holy motherfucking shit."

"If you're having a gay crisis, I don't want to hear about it."

"Merman."

"I swear to God... Jerry. What the hell?"

"He's a...he's a..." Jerry bounced. "Merman!"

"Are you broken?" I dug around for my phone. I was going to call Marcy.

Jerry grabbed my face, angled it toward the body, and shouted, "Merman!"

"I don't see any tail."

"Okay, but what about that?"

"That's a penis."

Oh.

It sure was.

Large. Thick.

Hard.

...Wait.

When had he rolled over? He was now lying flat to the dark and sodden sand. Hadn't he been on his side? And his leg, had it moved? Wasn't it hitched up, covering his groin, and weren't his arms...?

"That's an erection," Jerry corrected me. "Probably rigor mortis."

I couldn't swear to it, but I didn't think an erection was part of the rigor mortis experience. Then again, my forensic knowledge had been acquired while squinting at the screen during the obligatory morgue scene in every crime show ever filmed, and waiting for it to pass. What did I know?

"Anyway, I'm talking about this." Jerry squatted down again, his hold on my face taking me with him. And, coincidentally, putting me eye level with the penis.

Jerry squeezed my jaw and redirected my gaze.

"Is it just me," he said, "or does the dead guy have gills?"

ABOUT THE AUTHOR

Isabel Murray is a writer, a reader, and a lover of love. She couldn't stick to a subgenre if her life depended on it, but MM romance is her jam. She lives in the UK, reads way too much, and cannot be trusted anywhere near chocolate.

You can find Isabel at her website, or on Goodreads, Amazon, and Bookbub.

www.isabelmurrayauthor.wordpress.com

Printed in Great Britain
by Amazon